Fireside and Stone

The Fireside Mysteries: a cozy dragon mystery - book 2

K.E. O'Connor

K.E. O'Connor Books

FIRESIDE AND STONE

Copyright © 2023 by K.E. O'Connor

ISBN: 978-1-915378-73-6

Written by: K.E. O'Connor

*Article from the recently decommissioned Ithric
Times.*

By (the late) Norris Rippleton

Royal family denies dragons' return as extravagant royal wedding looms!

The Ithric realm has found itself embroiled in a swirl of rumors suggesting the return of the dragons that once graced the skies. The Royal Family, however, is quick to quash these speculations, emphasizing the importance of focusing on the upcoming royal wedding and the anticipation of a future heir.

The rumors gained traction in recent weeks, with whispers circulating through the kingdom about alleged signs of the dragons' return. The Royal Family, led by Lady Isolda Ithric, unequivocally denies these claims, urging the citizens to refrain from spreading baseless rumors that could sow discord.

In a brief statement issued by the royal court, Lady Isolda dismissed the rumors as unfounded and lacking credible evidence. "The realm remains steadfast, and such idle gossip distracts us from the joyous occasion that awaits us."

The Royal Family directed public attention to the upcoming wedding—a momentous event that will unite the kingdom in celebration. The wedding, a symbol of continuity and unity, is expected to be a joyous occasion.

However, the event is tempered by the absence of Prince Godric, who is currently representing the family at sea. The whereabouts of the headstrong younger prince has been a topic of speculation, with the Royal Family assuring the public his absence results from his duties in service to the realm.

They also expressed their hopes for the future, emphasizing the anticipation of a new generation and an heir to carry on the legacy of the Ithric bloodline. "Let us focus on the positive and look forward to the future," Lady Isolda stated.

As the Ithric Realm navigates the tide of speculation surrounding the dragons, the Royal Family remains steadfast in their commitment to stability, urging their citizens to set aside unfounded rumors and join in the celebration of the impending royal wedding.

A new article discovered in the Ithric Castle archives.

Author unknown

An anonymous informant and eyewitness accounts confirm recent dragon sightings in undisclosed locations. The evidence suggests these majestic creatures, once thought to be extinct in this area, are preparing for a comeback that could reshape the very fabric of the Ithric realm.

Mysterious roars have been heard echoing through the night, scorched landscapes have been discovered reminiscent of dragon fire breath, and an unusual surge in unexplained seismic activities has been recorded. The informant contends that the royal family, in an attempt to maintain control and quell public unrest, is suppressing the truth about the return of the dragons.

Despite the lack of concrete proof and the Royal Family's denial, the conspiracy theory has gained traction among those who believe. The return of these creatures has sparked excitement among the citizens.

As the rumors spread, speculation runs rampant about the dragons' impact on the realm.

The royal family urges the public to dismiss these theories and focus on the upcoming royal wedding, emphasizing unity and stability in the face of unfounded speculation.

While our rulers navigate this turbulent sea of rumors, only time will reveal whether the dragons are on the cusp of returning or if this theory is nothing more than a fantastical tale fueled by the desire for mystery and intrigue.

Do you believe the dragons are returning?

Chapter 1

The servants' tunnel in the castle was chilly, but I was happy to hide there with Hodgepodge and stay out of the way of the chaos inside the stone chamber.

"Here comes another one," Hodgepodge whispered in his soft Scottish lilt. "We should have been told this was happening."

I laughed softly and pressed a hand against his cool scaled side. "Why would the Ithric family tell us their business?"

"Because we run this chamber. This place would be nothing without us." Hodgepodge stamped his feet against my collarbone, his thick tail wrapped loosely around my neck as he glowered at the scene in front of us.

Four stoutly built ogres with bushy beards and bulging biceps wrestled with a life-sized stone statue. They were grunting and cursing as they hefted the sizable hunk of rock into position. This was the fifth statue they'd brought in tonight, and the chamber had been closed for two hours to visitors so the new additions could be added.

"Why would the family commission statues of people?" I asked. "Surely, they'd get more offerings if they added another dragon. It seems odd."

"Everything the family does is odd," Hodgepodge said. "It's best we don't question them. You just clean and stay out of their way as much as possible."

"Lady Isolda could have found a new hobby," I mused. "Alice said that part of Camilla's dowry has already been paid, even though she's not yet married Prince Jasper. That money will have gone into Lady Isolda's coffers, and she's already spending it."

"More fool her," Hodgepodge muttered.

"Watch out, you clod-footed moron!" One of the ogres shoved another, and they tussled while their companions struggled to keep the new statue they'd been hefting upright.

"Quit your scrapping and help us before this thing smashes!" a harassed-looking ogre grumbled. "And don't let Lady Isolda catch you messing around, or she'll have your worthless heads on poles. And I won't try to stop her."

That comment broke up the fight, and they returned to their duties. Everyone, no matter how large or powerful, feared the Ithric family. And they had a right to be feared. For a long time, I'd been ignorant of their underhanded activities, but my eyes had been opened to their deceit, and I knew the truth about the part they'd played in destroying the dragons who'd ruled this realm with them.

"This had better be the last one," the largest ogre said. "My stomach feels as if my throat's been slit, and you promised us dinner an hour ago."

"You'll get your meal, so long as we make it out of this creepy place alive." His companion headed to the giant statue of Emberthorn. He rudely poked the dragon's cheek. "These things smell strange."

"That's your armpits you're getting a whiff of. The stench makes me gag, too."

"Quit your yapping and come sniff him. He smells... earthy." The ogre leaned closer to Emberthorn and inhaled deeply.

I held my breath. It had been three weeks since I'd awoken Emberthorn and his brother, Stormwing, with my blood. Since then, I'd been working with Seraphina Poldark and a group of friends to get the dragons strong enough so they could escape the stone chamber. It was a daily battle to ensure they still looked like they were made of stone while we healed them. And while doing that, we had to ensure no one in the castle realized what we were up to. The Ithric family wouldn't hesitate to extinguish the dragons again. And they'd destroy us, too.

I stared closely at Emberthorn's enormous bulk. The family had created life-sized replicas of Emberthorn and Stormwing, so we needed an impressive amount of complicated magic to conceal their resurrection. Sometimes, the magic faltered.

"Is Emberthorn's tail twitching?" I whispered to Hodgepodge.

"I'd twitch too if I was stuck like that all day. They must be desperate to take flight."

"They will soon enough. Just so long as the ogres don't figure out something is amiss with our dragons and report it to a guard."

"No need to worry. Ogres have sensitive noses, so they could be getting a sniff of dragon scales. And Stormwing has been gassy for days. His wind is disgustingly pungent. And it lingers," Hodgepodge said.

"Enough with the sniffing, you creepy toad." The ogre who appeared to be in charge marched over and swatted his companion on the back of the head. In response, he turned and tackled him to the floor, and they rolled several times, kicking and biting each other.

The other ogres stopped working and laughed as they watched the tussle. I'd met a few ogres, so it wasn't alarming to see them fight. It was how they communicated. Rough play and coarse language meant they were comfortable with each other. Although I wasn't happy to see blood on the floor. I'd be the one scrubbing it off.

The ogres slammed into the base of one of the new statues and set it rocking. I gasped as the others grabbed for it just as Lady Isolda Ithric swept into the chamber, resplendent in a crimson dress with a matching floor-length robe trimmed with white ermine fur. She was a striking-looking woman, magically powerful, with a circlet of sparkling diamonds set in a tiara in her hair.

She watched the fight for a moment, her usual gaggle of cowering assistants around her. An assistant went to speak but ducked his head and cowered away, as if expecting to be struck when Lady Isolda held up a hand.

"Silence!" That word was like a giant ice shard slicing through the air and hitting the ogres. They stopped tussling and leapt to their feet. They stared at each other then fell to their knees and held their hands up.

"Forgive us," one of them said.

"We meant nothing by it. Nothing was damaged. We were just messing with each other."

"You hit a statue." Lady Isolda strode toward the kneeling ogres as their companions looked on with fear in their eyes. "What would have happened if it had fallen to the floor and smashed?"

They were wise enough not to answer that question.

"I didn't pay you to come into a sacred space and destroy it with bluster and ignorance." Lady Isolda circled the two kneeling ogres. "How dare you be so disrespectful."

More mumbled apologies filled the air. They stopped the instant Lady Isolda blasted a spell into one of the ogre's chests, sending him reeling. His companion flinched but remained on his knees.

Lady Isolda pointed at the wounded ogre. "Take that thing away and show it to your people. Let that be a lesson to never disrespect my home again."

The ogres jumped into action, dragging away their wounded companion and mumbling more apologies.

I wrinkled my nose. Lady Isolda knew how ogres behaved. They'd meant no disrespect. If they'd been quiet, that would have been disrespectful to the dragons, but the ogres had felt comfortable enough in Emberthorn and Stormwing's presence to be themselves. And I know Emberthorn would have approved. It was how dragons had always been. They encouraged magical creatures and magic users to be themselves.

It was the opposite way the Ithric family ruled the realm. The day after the dragons had been destroyed, the family issued a binding decree that only a select few could use magic. Everyone else was forbidden from using it or severely limited to basic spells.

"Lady Isolda is almost as bad as Prince Godric," Hodgepodge muttered.

I nodded. Prince Godric had been the twisted younger son of Lady Isolda. "At least we don't have to worry about him anymore."

"He's fish food," Hodgepodge said with a grunt of satisfaction. "And the fish are welcome to him. I don't expect he tasted good, though. Anyone so full of malice must leave a bitter aftertaste."

Prince Godric met a watery death after we'd done battle aboard a ship that was taking away the women he'd imprisoned. Unbeknownst to him, he hadn't needed to drain those women of blood. The dragons just needed a few drops of my blood to make them stir.

It was an understatement to say it was a shock and a half to discover I was linked to the dragons, and they'd chosen me to be their emissary. But ever since that day, things had changed. I'd found a purpose larger than my simple, safe life. It didn't mean I no longer craved a peaceful night in front of a roaring fire, a blanket on my lap, and Hodgepodge snuggled next to me while we read a book, but I had new obligations.

The world felt different. Scarily different, but I was committed to helping the dragons and setting them free, no matter what it took.

We watched in silence as Lady Isolda inspected each of the statues. Her assistants walked behind her, their bodies tense, knowing the wrong word, an incorrect answer to a question, or even breathing in a way that displeased Lady Isolda, would end in punishment.

"What's my next appointment?" she asked, directing her words in the general attention of her heel scurriers.

"You're having dinner with the Minister of Education," a pale-skinned, blond assistant said.

"That tedious little man. The food had better be excellent to make up for his dreadful company." Lady Isolda strode out of the chamber, barking orders at her assistants.

"It's safe to go back in," Hodgepodge said. "And it's nearly the top of the hour, so we'll be opening the doors again soon."

I collected my cleaning equipment and hurried into the stone chamber, heading for the statues. I cleaned as I went, marking spots where there was ogre blood so they'd be easy to come back to. I was inspecting the first face of the life-sized statue when the floor bucked. It was a signal I was waiting for.

I dashed to Emberthorn. I curtsied before him then rested my hand on his face. "Those ogres sensed something about you. We're getting close."

"My skin is itching," he grumbled.

"There's nothing worse than an itch you can't scratch," Hodgepodge said. "I can never get to the base of my tail. I always have to get Bell to do it for me."

I gave Hodgepodge a quick scratch. "I'm happy to do it. And I'll do it for you too, with your permission. Although we'll need something bigger than my hands to get all of you."

"Anything! I'm in desperate need of relief." Emberthorn's voice was a low grumbled growl. It was the dragon version of a whisper.

I hunted through my cleaning equipment and pulled out a large stiff-bristled brush. "Where does it itch?"

"Everywhere!" A plume of smoke wafted out of Emberthorn's enormous nostrils.

I smiled and raised my eyebrows. It wasn't like Emberthorn to be grouchy, but I'd be the same if I'd been stuck in stone form for years and then, when I awoke, I was too weak to move.

"I'll start at the back and work forward. But I don't have long," I said.

He groaned, and the floor shook again as I set to work on his rear. "You're an angel sent to us."

I grinned as I tackled his left back foot, working the brush into the stone grooves of his claws. Although there was strong concealment magic covering both dragons, when I looked closely, I saw a brief flash of magnificent scales beneath the stone. I was so excited about the prospect of the dragons returning. It would change everything in the realm.

"Your hiding place in the forest is ready," I said. "When you're strong enough to fly, we'll head there. Then you can rest and recover."

"I'll be grateful to leave. I don't like the new additions in the chamber."

I chuckled. "You're worried the visitors will be more interested in them than you?"

Emberthorn rumbled a laugh, and a brief plume of smoke shot into the air. "It's not that. I sense magic in them. Dragon magic."

I paused my vigorous scrubbing and glanced at the new statues. "Huh! Why would a dragon create stone statues with their magic?"

"It's unlikely they would, unless they were being forced to do so. The statues serve no purpose."

"It's a puzzle, but it's not one we're going near," Hodgepodge said. "We have enough on our plate saving your scaled behinds."

Life had been busy since I'd awoken the dragons, so I didn't disagree with Hodgepodge.

I scrubbed Emberthorn for two minutes. "That'll have to do. I need to clean the ogre blood off the floor before the visitors descend upon you."

"I feel much better. Thank you, Bell." The floor stopped shaking, revealing Emberthorn's mood had improved.

I took a few minutes to clean the mess the ogres had left behind then took a final peek at a new statue. "This one looks like the gate guard, Saunders. Is Lady Isolda having staff replicas made?"

"If she is, she'd start with her family rather than her gate guards," Hodgepodge said. "I doubt she even acknowledges the guards' existence. But we have no time to consider what our unstable ruler is up to. I can hear the crowd outside getting restless. They're not used to the chamber being closed for so long."

The main door that let in visitors opened, and a guard popped his head in. "All set?"

I grabbed my cleaning things and nodded then dashed back to the servants' tunnels with Hodgepodge, and we slid inside.

The addition of the new statues was a puzzle I'd solve another time. My focus was on the dragons.

Chapter 2

I wearily pushed open the door to my small lodgings set behind the stables close to the Ithric castle. I raised a hand to Griffin Alvarez and Evander Thorne. I was so used to seeing them turning up uninvited that it was no longer a surprise when I discovered they'd made themselves at home. Nor was it surprising Evander was lounging in the only comfortable chair in the place, while Griffin was at work in the kitchen.

"I thought you might appreciate being looked after." Griffin was useful in the kitchen and always made excellent stew.

"I look after Bell. She doesn't need anyone else poking their noses into our lives." Hodgepodge curled himself around my neck.

"You're welcome to cook, lizard," Evander said. "But even with only one arm, Griffin is better in the kitchen than you'll ever be."

Hodgepodge hissed at him.

"Have you heard about the new arrivals in the chamber?" I unclipped my cloak and hung it on the small peg by the door.

"It's all everyone's talking about." Evander flashed me a handsome smile and finally rolled out of my seat. "Take the weight off. I was warming it for you."

"Sure you were." I didn't hesitate to drop into the seat and groan my relief. I was bone-weary, having worked since dawn, and it was now just gone midnight.

"I saw some of the statues being brought in," Griffin said. "The ogres got lost and needed directions while I was in the yard."

"Did you get a good look at them?" I stretched out my legs and settled Hodgepodge on my lap.

"No. They were covered," Griffin said. "I asked where they came from but just got grunted at."

"It's the oddest thing. While I was cleaning, I inspected each one. They look like people who work in the castle." I eased off my boots and rolled my socked feet on a smooth stone I kept under the chair for just such a reason.

"I wouldn't mind being immortalized in stone." Evander poured mead for us and handed around the mugs. "I'm sure there are plenty of ladies I've enchanted over the years who'd be happy to see my striking image every day."

"To cover in graffiti and insult because you charmed them and then used them," Griffin said.

"It's not using when there's a mutual understanding involved."

Evander was a handsome devil, and he knew it. He had no reluctance about exploiting his charms to get what he wanted. And it served him well. He owned one of the cutest little places in the center of the village, had contacts in every town, and an enormous wardrobe of tailored tunics that fitted him perfectly.

Griffin grumbled to himself as he passed around bowls of stew. "I wouldn't want a statue made of me. There's no one here who'd want to remember me, anyway."

Griffin's ego had never recovered, following a spectacular fall from grace. He'd been an elite member of the royal guard, but when the family was attacked while traveling, their possessions had been stolen. Not a single member of the family had been hurt, Griffin made sure of that, but in the fight, he'd been injured and had lost an arm. Rather than being rewarded by the family, they'd punished him for losing their things, refusing him treatment, and stripping him of all privileges. He now spent his days in the yard, doing menial work and mucking out the horses.

"I'd want to see your statue," I said. "I'd visit at least once a week."

"You wouldn't want to see it if it was scowling like the real thing," Evander said.

"None of us are important enough to have a statue made of us." Hodgepodge inspected the stew in my bowl. "We should be grateful for that. It's vital we remain unremarkable and quiet."

"Our quiet days are numbered." Evander leaned against the kitchen counter while he ate the stew. "How are the dragons?"

"It's nearly time to move them." Excitement flickered inside me like a tickle of dragon fire. Ever since they'd returned, I'd worked tirelessly with my friends to ensure we could get the dragons safely out of the castle and to a secure hiding spot. "Emberthorn was complaining about how itchy he felt today."

"Poor guy, stuck like that, not able to move," Evander said.

"Seraphina is doing a great job with the restorative magic. Spells that powerful take time. The magic that trapped the dragons was laced through with darkness," I said.

Evander grunted. "She should know since she helped the family trap them in the first place."

"Something she's working hard to make amends for." I scooped up stew.

"Seraphina stopped by earlier," Griffin said. "She left you more enchanted stones and another vial of potion. She said one stone per dragon and two drops of potion every day before noon."

I nodded. It was the usual routine. "How did she seem?"

"Exhausted. I don't think she's sleeping," Griffin said.

"Because the guilt is eating her alive," Evander said.

"Emberthorn has forgiven her, although I'm not so sure about Stormwing. He growls every time she gets too close." It was why I'd been given the task of administering regular doses of healing magic to both dragons. Emberthorn was generally amenable, but Stormwing was grouchy and dour. He was always blowing acrid smoke into Seraphina's face and making her choke.

"Have you both looked over the roster I set up?" I asked. "Once the dragons are free, someone will need to be with them all the time. They'll be vulnerable until they're strong enough to defend themselves. I don't know how long it'll be until they can breathe fire again."

"It looked good to me," Evander said. "And I'm grateful you didn't give me early shifts."

"We all know you're a layabout who doesn't get out of bed before noon," Griffin said.

"There's no need to. Unlike some around here, I don't have horse dung to tackle. The royal horses get aggrieved if their dung isn't removed the second they take a—"

"We all play our part," I said.

"You shouldn't be on the roster," Griffin said to me. "You work long hours at the castle and need rest."

"I'm taking shifts just like everyone else."

Evander chuckled. "No offense, Bell, but how will you defend the dragons if someone creeps up in the middle of the night and tries to harm them? Bore them to death with cleaning tips?"

"I can fight!" I had magic, but its lack of use made my spells rusty and sluggish. "I still have Elara's ring of strength. You know from personal experience how effective that can be."

Evander grimaced while Griffin laughed.

"Besides, I want to be there," I said. "The dragons trust me not to hurt them."

"So they should," Griffin said. "You're their emissary, and you've been nothing but kind to them. You believed in them when no one else did."

"I always believed in the dragons," Evander said. "I'm especially looking forward to the rich rewards they give me to show their gratitude for my heroic deeds."

"I'm sure that'll be top of their priorities once they're free." Griffin shook his head and pursed his lips. "Bell, does Evander have to be involved?"

"Yes! Between us, we can do this. But we must work together," I said. "No one at the castle can get suspicious about what we're doing. That'll involve teamwork."

"The royal family thrives on remaining suspicious," Evander said. "It's the only way they've stayed alive so long. Although, did you hear about the rioting close to the swamp land? Unrest grows daily."

I sighed. "It doesn't surprise me. The more I hear about how the family isn't looking after the realm, the more surprised I am that towns and villages aren't defying them and demanding better treatment. It's no less than they deserve."

Those who lived close to the Ithric Castle saw prosperity and showy displays of wealth. The ministers, their families, and influential royal aides lived in expensive houses and were free to use magic. But you didn't have to edge far from this insular environment to realize the smaller towns and villages were ignored. The royal family chose to sweep disputes under the carpet. If the Ithric family couldn't see the problem, then they didn't believe it was real. They rarely ventured outside of the sturdy castle walls to see what a mess they'd made of the realm they were supposed to protect.

There was a sharp tap on the door. Astrid Nightshade sauntered in, her dirty blonde hair pulled off her face. "Hey! The gang is back together."

"You're late," Griffin said.

She set a white box on the kitchen counter and blew him a kiss. "I was getting dessert. Evander said it was my turn."

"Stole it, did you?" Evander dodged a punch on the arm and lifted the lid of the box.

"I can pay my way when I need to. But I don't often need to." Astrid grinned at me. She was a gifted troublemaker and an astonishingly astute tracker. She was tiny, quick on her feet, and used illegal magic to get away with crimes most people wouldn't dare to attempt.

"Hold on. I know this cake. Isn't this a layer from Prince Jasper's wedding cake?" Evander stared into the box with wide eyes. "There are pictures of the wretched thing everywhere."

"Maybe it is. Maybe it isn't. All we've been hearing about is that darn wedding and how it's gonna change everything," Astrid said. "They made such a ridiculous show of the oh-so-happy couple stuffing their faces with cake. It was on the front page of the newspaper. It's a no-news story if ever I've seen one."

"It couldn't have been that meaningless to you since you know about it," Griffin said.

"I know about the staggering amount of waste it cost a friend of mine. They forced Georgia to close her bakery for a week and do nothing but bake cake samples. She lost so much business. And do you think she got paid?" Astrid shook her head. "And then Camilla complained of having an upset stomach and didn't want to eat anything. Georgia was almost in tears over the amount of cake that would be dumped. She was thinking of auctioning it off, but I decided we should enjoy a few slices. This layer won't be missed."

"It's red velvet," Evander said. "My favorite."

"I prefer pie," Hodgepodge said.

Astrid strode over and tickled him on the top of his head. "And pie you shall have, my adorable lizard. I never forget you." She pulled a small brown paper bag from an inside jacket pocket. "It's squashed, but it'll still be tasty."

We gathered around the box of cake and divided up the dessert.

"We were just talking about the dragon roster," I said to Astrid.

"Is that so? I thought you'd have been talking about gorgeous angels."

I tilted my head. "Why would we do that?"

Astrid's grin widened. "I know your secret, Bell Blackthorn. You put on this innocent act, but I knew there was more to you than that."

"Um... My secret? What secret am I supposed to be keeping?"

"Bell doesn't have any secrets," Hodgepodge said. "We share everything."

"I'm talking about your secret boyfriend." Astrid waggled her eyebrows.

"I'm forty! I'm too old for boys or boyfriends. I don't even know what I'd call any guy I dated. Guy friend? Man friend? Anyway, I don't have one."

Astrid laughed. "Whatever. Your man friend. Paramor. Bed mate. He's here."

"Bell's been dating on the sly?" Evander placed a hand over his heart. "I thought you were waiting for me?"

I swatted his arm with the back of my hand. "I'd have to get on the end of a very long line if I wanted to date you."

Evander roared out a laugh. "It's true. And there's only so much of me to go around."

"I don't see that queue anywhere," Astrid said. "You must be thinking of the line of women scurrying away from Evander because they want nothing to do with a no-good toerag who steals pennies from street dogs."

"Street dogs carry pennies?" Griffin asked.

We all laughed, but I didn't miss the flash of wounded pride that crossed Evander's face. He may be a rogue, but he was a noble one.

"You're seeing someone?" Griffin asked me.

"No. I haven't dated anyone in an age. The last date I had ended up with the guy getting food poisoning. I think he blamed me, even though he chose the place to eat," I said.

"This one is cute," Astrid said. "But then I've never met an angel who wasn't on the right side of yum, with a side order of 'OMG get me a huge fan because it's getting hot in here'."

Hodgepodge gulped down a piece of squashed pie. He growled and flicked his tail. "It had better not be who I think it is."

I glanced at him. "Who do you think it is?"

"You really don't know he's here?" Astrid asked. "I hope it's not meant to be a surprise that I've just ruined."

"I'm not expecting any visitors," I said.

Her smile faded, and her hand went to the hilt of a blade tucked into her custom-made belt. "If this angel is stalking you, let me know, and I'll run him out of the realm."

"I'm in the dark about this. Who do you think I'm secretly dating or being stalked by?"

Astrid ate a huge mouthful of wedding cake, and I glowered at her as she chewed and grinned at my obvious frustration. She finally finished her mouthful. "I was out late this afternoon, minding my own business, seeing if there was any fun to be had, when I heard someone asking about you. He said he was looking for Bell Blackthorn and you were friends."

Hodgepodge hissed. "No! He's not welcome here."

"Hodgie, who do you think it is?" I asked.

"That wretched angel creature from Crimson Cove!"

My mouth dropped open, my heartbeat sped up, and my eyes widened.

Astrid laughed. "There it is! The penny has dropped. You've bagged yourself a super-hot angel hunk. He called himself Finn."

Chapter 3

The large stone castle corridor was cold with a dash of gray bleak as I sped along it with Hodgepodge wrapped around my neck. "I still can't figure out what Finn is doing here."

"Can we stop talking about the dubious angel?" Hodgepodge huffed in my ear. "You thought of nothing else all night. No good will come of his visit."

"Angels are good. They wouldn't be in charge of law enforcement in most places if they couldn't be trusted." The castle was barely stirring, with most people fortunate enough to be in bed at this early hour, so we had the place to ourselves. When it was quiet like this, I liked to imagine what life would be like if we owned such a place. For starters, it would be much warmer. But this morning, I was distracted from my fantasy home décor activities by an angel.

Hodgepodge huffed hot breath in my ear. "Ignore Finn! Get tangled up with him, and it'll lead to trouble."

"What trouble could he cause?" I stopped to pick up scatter cushions that had been tossed on the floor and set them back on the chairs.

"You've forgotten he's not just an angel? There's a hefty amount of demon inside him. There's never anything good about demons."

"I've never met one. They've been outlawed around here ever since the dragons were silenced." I hurried to my cleaning closet and pulled out my supplies.

"Which is even more reason why we should have nothing to do with Finn," Hodgepodge said. "He's not supposed to be here, and the Ithric family will hate you associating with him. It'll make them suspicious of you."

"They won't notice I'm speaking to Finn."

"They'll notice a hulking great angel striding around this tiny village. We're supposed to keep things quiet and not draw attention to ourselves. Remember, we must keep the dragons safe."

I slid him some side-eye. "Don't use my devotion to the dragons against me. I'll do anything to protect Emberthorn and Stormwing, but there's no harm in finding out what Finn is doing here. I like him. He's kind and funny."

"And he makes you blush every time you see him. I don't approve. He's not safe to be around. Forget Astrid ever mentioned Finn. He's probably left by now, anyway."

"He was asking around for me. He'll find me, eventually."

"That doesn't mean you have to meet with him. I imagine red flags every time I think about that angel-demon." Hodgepodge hissed at nothing, although I could imagine him picturing Finn standing in front of us.

After Astrid had revealed the surprising news Finn was in the area, I'd had a restless night. I did want to see him again, but there was so much going on. If Finn had come here hoping to see the tourist spots and enjoy leisurely lunches with me, he'd be disappointed.

"You're still thinking about him." Hodgepodge nipped my ear with his teeth.

"Partly, but I'm mainly thinking about how our lives have gotten so complicated. The only tricky thing we used to have to consider was what type of cookie to have with our hot cocoa in the evening."

"Those were the days. Let's hope we get back to them soon."

I hoped for that, too, but didn't see a return to our peaceful lives for some time.

I entered the quiet calm of the stone chamber. Four more life-sized statues had arrived overnight. I hurried over to inspect them. "Two of these statues look familiar. I've seen the people they're modeled on around the village."

"I've definitely seen this guy. He works in the weapons room. Something to do with magical armor for the guards," Hodgepodge said. "He's always strutting around and has that braying laugh that grates down my spine like a ragged fingernail."

"You're right. Wow! The likeness is extraordinary." I peered at the rest of the statues. Whoever was designing them had skill and must have worked for many years to become so talented. "This one is grimacing. Almost like he was in pain when the sculptor worked on his image."

"He looks surprised to me," Hodgepodge said. "Maybe that's the face he pulled when he was posing."

"I was hoping to see Saunders at the gate this morning," I said. "I wanted to ask him about being immortalized in stone. He's usually on duty during the week, isn't he?"

"He was probably late for work. Don't bother the guards. They'll only get interested in you and ask questions we don't want to answer."

"Some of them are okay. If we have time, I'll ask them how Saunders got his lucky break. Maybe the family is commissioning a representative from different factions in the castle. I wonder which servant they'll choose. It should be Alice. She always has the kitchen running so smoothly."

"So long as it's not us, I don't care," Hodgepodge said.

"You don't think I'd make a magnificent statue?" I posed beside the statue of a frowning woman.

"You'd make the perfect statue. Everyone would stare and want to know your name. Do you really want to be the center of attention?"

I shook my head. "I'll politely decline when I'm asked."

"You do that. Now, hurry. We only have ten minutes before the doors open. You check the dragons. I'll check for dirt. No doubt some clumpy foot made a mess when bringing the new statues in." Hodgepodge jumped off my shoulder and hurried away.

I walked to Emberthorn, happy to see him asleep. Seraphina's magic was doing its job. Both dragons would heal faster with plenty of rest, and with Emberthorn snoozing, it meant he wouldn't complain about feeling itchy.

Stormwing was also slumbering, so I left them to it and continued my cleaning duties.

"Bell! Get over here."

The worried tone in Hodgepodge's voice had me speed-walking around Emberthorn. As I rounded his flank, my eyes widened at the devastation. A life-sized statue had been destroyed. There were chunks of stone scattered everywhere. "How did this happen?"

"Must have been damaged when the new ones arrived." Hodgepodge was sniffing around the broken statue. "This smells strange. Like bitter lemon and something even sharper."

"It would have taken more than a gentle shove to knock that over. I almost broke a toe when I accidentally kicked one yesterday."

Hodgepodge looked up at me. "You don't think this was an accident?"

"Maybe. If the ogres delivered the last lot and they weren't looking where they were going, they could have bashed into another statue hard enough to knock it off balance. You'd think they'd clear up the evidence, though." I picked up a piece of the stone. It was oddly warm. "They know what Lady Isolda would do if she discovered this."

"They must have panicked. Realized their heads would be on the chopping block, so they fled."

I looked at the remaining statues. "Wasn't this statue of Augustus Doubleday? One of Prince Godric's aides."

Hodgepodge checked the other statues on either side. "I reckon so. Unless they moved them around last night, and there'd be no reason for them to do that."

"Oh, dear. What have we stumbled upon?" a male voice said behind me.

I froze then turned to the door and curtsied low. Prince Jasper Ithric and his fiancée, Camilla Oldsbrook, stood in the open doorway at the back of the chamber. I'd been so focused on the destroyed statue that I hadn't heard the door open. I remained in a curtsy and kept my head down.

"Did you do this?" Prince Jasper strode over, Camilla lagging behind him, dressed in a form-fitting cream dress, the hem at the back extended, so it trailed the floor like a wedding veil.

"No, your Royal Highness. I arrived for work and discovered the broken statue." I held my skirts wide, giving Hodgepodge time to hide. I couldn't see him, so he must have ducked behind one of the other statues.

"What a dreadful mess." Prince Jasper was the taller of the two Ithric princes. He had the same high cheekbones and cold eyes of his mother, but his mouth was fuller, and he smiled more. "Don't you think it's a shame, Camilla?"

She murmured a reply so softly, I didn't catch it. She looked pale, dark circles sitting under her eyes, distracting from her elf-like beauty.

"You must have given it a hearty whack with that bucket to send it tumbling," Prince Jasper said.

"Forgive me, sir, but I doubt I'd be able to shove it over even if I meant to," I said. "They're heavy. It took four ogres to bring the first batch in."

"Fascinating. And which one was this?" Prince Jasper kicked a piece of stone.

"I believe it was the replica of Augustus Doubleday, Prince Godric's assistant."

"Oh! Augustus. He works for me now," Prince Jasper said. "I can't say I trust the fella, though. He let my brother get away with far too much. Perhaps you'd like him on your staff, Camilla. He's biddable."

She didn't reply, her gaze fixed on the broken stone.

"Well? I just offered you a valuable member of staff. The least you could do is thank me."

"Thank you," she whispered. "I don't need staff, though. I have my own. They'll be arriving soon."

"You can always have more. He's a reliable type. Tells you everything you want to hear. Of course, my brother would never hire anyone who spoke against him," Prince Jasper said. "When he returns from his adventure at sea, I expect he'll have a new team for us to whip into shape. Salty seadogs who drink too much, no doubt."

I risked a glance at Prince Jasper. So far, everyone believed the story about Prince Godric being seen at the docks looking for passage on board a ship. I'd even cultivated whispers among the women I'd helped rescue that he'd lost his mind and believed he was a sailor. The idea wasn't far-fetched, given the mental frailties his father displayed, currently confined to a castle turret, and only glimpsed at the high narrow windows, peering out at the realm he once ruled.

Prince Jasper rested his hands on his hips and looked around the chamber. "I find the statues creepy. Especially the dragons. I always feel as if I'm being watched when I'm in here."

"They're beautiful," Camilla said.

Prince Jasper's cheery expression hardened. "Of course. Anything I despise, you like. Why am I not surprised?"

I pretended I hadn't heard his comment. "Would you like me to clear away the broken statue? Visitors will arrive soon."

"Do what you like. I have no interest in these ugly creations. Still, I suppose my mother will disapprove if her precious statues look out of place. Less money for the coffers if the visitors are unhappy."

I kept my head down and nodded.

"Come now. You two act as if I have a sparking staff in my hand and have threatened to obliterate you. I'm not a monster!" Prince Jasper sighed. "My family can be peculiar, but I'm not like them. Having spent time away from this morbid, dreary castle, I know there's a different world out there. A better one. And with my brother enjoying life on the open waves, things are improving. Don't you agree, Camilla?"

I lifted my head when Camilla didn't speak, and her gaze met mine. There was fear in her eyes.

"I don't know why I bother. I'm attempting to be pleasant, yet you treat me like I'm about to give you fifty lashes." Prince Jasper huffed out his dissatisfaction. "Clear this mess, and I won't tell if you don't."

I stared at him with surprise. What did he mean? "I should report the damage."

"And get yourself in trouble with my dear mother? No, no, no. There's no need for that. We'll fix things and say no more. Then you'll owe me a small favor. How does that sound?"

It sounded horrific. I didn't want to be in debt to anyone in the royal family.

The floor gently shook beneath our feet, and a grumble rippled through the air. It sounded like thunder, but I knew where the noise was coming from.

"What was that? Sounded like thunder, but the room wobbled. How peculiar. It had better not be an earthquake. Come, my love. Mother expects us for an early breakfast before we set out on our dutiful tour. Keep the peasants happy, eh?" Prince Jasper extended his elbow, and after a second of hesitation, Camilla took it. "Get to work dealing with that mess," he called over his shoulder as he retreated from the chamber.

"Thanks, Emberthorn," I whispered the second the door closed.

He gently puffed smoke out of his nostrils. "It was my pleasure. Prince Jasper needed distracting. I don't want you making deals with any members of this family, and that one is as slippery as an eel that's been soaked in olive oil. Don't fall for his charming smile. There's a vicious tongue concealed beneath the friendly veneer."

"Bell is far too sensible for that." Hodgepodge emerged from behind the statue he'd been using as cover.

"I know Bell has a good head on her shoulders," Emberthorn said, "but Prince Jasper always plays the nice card. He lulls people into a false sense of security and then bites. He's nastier than a dragon who's got an abscess on his tail."

"Camilla is terrified of him." I grabbed a broom and swept the smaller chunks of the statue into a large pile.

"You don't have time to pick it all up by hand," Hodgepodge said. "Use magic. No one will see."

I checked the time. There was less than five minutes until the doors opened to the public. Desperate times call for desperate measures and illegal magic.

"Go fetch Griffin," I said to Hodgepodge. "He'll have a wheelbarrow we can use."

Hodgepodge skittered away, and I finished gathering as much of the stone as I could. I flexed my fingers and twisted my wrists. Everyone had the ability to cast magic, but I'd gotten so used to hiding my magic that it felt alien to use it. But it was there, simmering below the surface, desperate to come out.

"You have nothing to fear," Emberthorn said softly. "Magic is in your veins. Pure, honest power. You'll only ever use it for good."

I closed my eyes and drew in a deep breath. On the exhale, I breathed out my desire. The largest pieces of stone shifted and slid toward me. Within a few seconds, all the pieces of the statue were in a large heap. Except one. A small piece that hadn't moved.

I dispersed my spell and hurried over to pick it up. It wasn't a piece of the statue. It was a small stone with rune marks cut into it.

The door at the back of the chamber opened, and Griffin hurried in, pushing a sturdy wheelbarrow. He'd adapted it so it had a single handle, making it easier for him to use.

"What's been going on?" he asked, nodding his head at the smashed statue.

"Thanks for coming. No time to explain." I thrust out another spell and a heap of stone dumped into the barrow. "I'll hide the larger pieces in the servants' tunnel, and we can come back for them later. Get rid of that for me."

"Of course. I'll store it in a shed." Griffin had already turned and was pushing the loaded barrow away. "Hodgepodge said you found it like that."

I nodded as I magicked the bigger stones into the tunnel. "Someone either had an accident, or they hated Augustus's statue enough to destroy it."

The main door opened, and a guard looked in. I gave him a thumbs-up, whispering another thank you to Emberthorn as I left the chamber, concealing the chunks of statue behind the door. That was a close call. Dealing with Prince Jasper and a destroyed statue first thing in the morning with barely any caffeine running through my veins was enough to test anyone's nerves. But at least it had stopped me from thinking about Finn.

Chapter 4

I slowly ate a delicious piece of tart blueberry pie as I walked around the busy marketplace. I wasn't trying to kid myself. I was looking for Finn. And I'd been looking for him every time I'd had a break from cleaning.

"If you're not eating that, I have a hole in my belly that needs filling." Hodgepodge had curled himself around my middle, using his tail like a belt on my waist and latching his claws into the front of my dress so he looked like an enormous, scaled brooch. It meant his head was directly underneath my mouth so he could catch falling pie crumbs.

"I'm just taking the air and not rushing my food. I want to enjoy every mouthful." I fed him a soft blueberry.

"You're looking for trouble. Don't do it. We're happy as we are. We occasionally let people into our lives, like Griffin, when we're hungry. Evander, when we need something. And Astrid... well, there's no reason to have Astrid in our lives, but we can't seem to get rid of her."

"If Astrid wasn't around, you'd miss her belly rubs."

"I would miss those. She can stay. We don't need anyone else permanently, though. Just the two of us is perfect."

"I don't disagree, but it's not as if Finn's seeking my hand in marriage. He's just being polite by looking me up while he's in the area."

"He wants something from you. Something you shouldn't give him."

"I'll only share my fruit pies with you. How's that for a bargain?"

Hodgepodge grunted. "I bet he eats a lot of pie. He's enormous. And I expect flying around and showing off those giant wings burns plenty of energy."

I grinned. "I'd like to see Finn fly."

Hodgepodge grumbled to himself. "Remember, we like a quiet life."

"It's a bit late for that," I said. "We're in the messy middle of a situation that's the opposite of quiet."

"Then we don't need to add more noise. Especially not angel-demon noise."

Hodgepodge had a point. I had to focus on the dragons and keep away from the Ithric family's attention. But I was excited to see Finn again. He hadn't dismissed me because I was only a castle cleaner. It was nice to meet someone who didn't judge me the second they knew about my lowly position.

I bit into the pie, and it crumbled in my hand, so I had no choice but to shove most of it into my mouth. Hodgepodge got the rest.

"There's one of the gate guards," I mumbled around my giant mouthful of sweet fruit and delicious pastry. "Let's ask about Saunders and his new statue."

"Bell! There you are. I've been looking everywhere for you."

I turned. And there he was. Finn was even more handsome than I remembered. He wasn't dressed in his usual Angel Force white uniform. He had on a brown tunic and a matching pair of trousers. I expected him to be wearing something more modern, considering where he came from, but he must be dressing to blend in. His wings were still on display, though, and they were drawing attention. Not that Finn noticed. His warm gaze was fixed on me as he strode over. His grin widened as I gulped down the last of the pie, almost choking in my haste to swallow.

"You've got a little something at the corner of your mouth." Finn gestured at my face, his sandy brown hair a perfect tangle.

I blushed and swiped a handkerchief across my lips. "Blueberry pie. Delicious but messy to eat while walking."

His smile grew a touch wicked. "I can tell it was blueberry."

Ground open and swallow me whole. What had I been thinking, wandering around, stuffing my face with pie while looking for Finn? Of course, this was going to happen.

"It looked like a delicious pie," Finn said. "I think I'll get a slice. Do you want to show me where you got it from?"

"You're not here for pie," Hodgepodge said. "What are you doing in our village?"

"It's nice to see you again, Hodgepodge. Would you like your own slice of pie? My treat," Finn said.

"He can only have a small amount of fruit or he gets an upset stomach and makes a mess. And the gas!" I waved a hand in front of my face.

Finn laughed. "Got it. No pie for Hodgepodge."

Hodgepodge hissed. "That was one time I got gas. I can manage a whole slice to myself."

"No! You had the squits for days." Why was I still talking about Hodgepodge's toileting habits?

"Shall we?" Finn gestured at the stalls. "This market has me all turned around, and I'm not sure where I've already been. It's so busy."

"I didn't think an angel would have a bad sense of direction," Hodgepodge said. "It must make flying hard."

"It does. And I don't enjoy flying."

"You don't?" I asked. "I thought all angels loved to fly."

"Not the ones who hate the cold." He pointed again at the stalls and dodged a group of chattering women, several of whom gave him admiring glances.

I deliberately forced myself not to smile to avoid exposing my blue teeth and nodded. "The cake stall is this way. They make amazing pies. Freshly baked every day. A friend introduced me to them. I can't really afford it, but I keep going back."

"They sound delicious." Finn fell into step with me. "You're a hard woman to track down. I've been asking around about you since I arrived yesterday. Most people didn't know anyone called Bell Blackthorn, though a few of the women I spoke to seemed familiar with your name. Suspicious, though, and they ended up asking me more questions than I did them. None of them would reveal where you lived."

"Nor should they," Hodgepodge said. "You're a stranger to them. Practically a stranger to us, too."

"Be nice, Hodgie," I said. "Finn's a friend. We've helped each other out."

"I like to think we're friends. New friends. And new friendships need cultivating. Is this the place?" Finn pointed at the cake stand.

I nodded. "The best pie in the realm. Well, not that I've tasted every pie from every bakery across the entire realm. That would be impossible, and it would take years. Not that I wouldn't be up for the challenge. Pie is my favorite food. Did I already say that?"

Finn chuckled. "I understand your love of pie. Would you like another slice of blueberry?"

I did want more pie. "I could go for some cherry, just to add a different color of stain to my fingers."

"Cherry it is." He ordered two large slices of cherry pie and carried them to a table for us to sit at. "Surprised to see me?"

"I am!" I set about my dessert slightly less vigorously, but it was always hard to be restrained around pie. "I heard from a friend last night that you were in the area."

Finn nodded. "Good. I figured word would get back to you that I was asking around. I hoped you'd look for me if you wanted to hook up."

"Bell doesn't hook up with anyone," Hodgepodge said. "She's not that kind of woman."

Finn laughed and shook his head. "Not that kind of hooking up. Catching up. I'm in the area following a lead, and I thought it would be nice to see a friendly face."

"It is nice. Surprisingly nice. You're working a case, then?" I felt a little disappointed that Finn hadn't come all this way just to see me. But why would he? We hadn't gotten close when we'd met during a murder investigation in Crimson Cove.

"This is an unofficial investigation," Finn said. "Strictly off the books. I'm on a quest."

"We hate quests," Hodgepodge said. "We got dragged into one recently, and we detested it. Quests are for idiots who enjoy throwing themselves into unnecessarily dangerous situations. Are you an idiot, Finn?"

"It depends on how much caffeine I've had. Most quests come with a certain amount of danger," Finn said. "What did your quest involve?"

"I'm more interested in yours," I said. "Perhaps we can help."

"No help," Hodgepodge said. "We don't have time to help anyone else. Remember, we're very busy helping others."

I bit my bottom lip. I liked Finn, but I didn't know him well, so I wouldn't be sharing my secrets with him. "Life has been busy since our brief visit to Crimson Cove. I'm just taking a break from work."

"At the castle," Finn said. "I remember."

"In the stone chamber," Hodgepodge said. "Cleaning. It's boring. You can't be interested in Bell's life."

"It can be dull work," I said. "Tell us what you're here for, though. I've lived here all my life, so I know most people and can point you in the right direction."

Hodgepodge sat alert on my lap, glaring at Finn.

Finn shrugged. "My quest isn't a secret. My dad got in touch a while back. Well, he claimed to be my dad."

"You don't know your own father?" Hodgepodge asked.

"Nope. I was given up when I was young. Angels are weird about the whole mishmash of magic thing. Most of them don't like their children to have demon magic mingled with angel."

"I'm sorry to hear that," I said. "I don't know much about angels, but there are a few magical species around here that are odd about that sort of thing, too."

"Yeah, angels are super odd. Put them at the number one spot for being odd about their kids needing to be perfectly angelic."

"I'd be suspicious if my child had a demon in him," Hodgepodge said.

"Hush now, Hodgie. That's not polite," I said. "So, your biological dad got in touch?"

"He said he wanted to reunite. It was going well, but long story short, I got framed for his murder. Juno and Zandra made everything right. They found the killer and got me free."

"Gosh! That's quite a story," I said. "I'd love to hear all about it."

"Definitely. Another time, though," Finn said. "Anyway, I got curious about where I came from. I know so little about my biological family, so I decided to find out about them. I started with the dad who showed up in Crimson Cove and soon learned he was a fake and pretending to be my father. My actual dad died in a messy fight years ago. And he was a terrible dude, so I'm glad I never had him in my life."

"I'm sorry to hear that, too," I said.

"Don't be. We had no connection. But I am still looking for my mother. She's an angel. A lead brought me close to here, and I figured while I was in the area, I'd look you up. I'm glad I did. This cherry pie is incredible."

"It is great pie," I said. "What about your job at Angel Force?"

"It's covered. My boss gave me a month off. She's in a good mood because she recently got married. And I've got enough volunteers to cover at the animal sanctuary, too. It'll give me time to look around. And I'm finding this place fascinating. It couldn't be any more different from Crimson Cove."

"The castle is something else, isn't it?" I said.

"Sure. And the statue park. I've seen nothing like it," Finn said.

"We have a statue park?" Hodgepodge asked. "When did that show up?"

"I've never seen it," I said.

"They were bringing several statues in while I watched. I was walking around looking at them, but I got kicked out by a surly guard. He said the statues belong to the family." Finn glanced at the castle. "I'm guessing he meant the ruling family?"

"We have had new additions to the stone chamber," I said. "But it's the first I've heard about a new statue park. Where is it?"

"I can show you if you like," Finn said. "If you don't have to rush back to work."

"We do," Hodgepodge said.

I checked the time. "Don't be so grumpy. We have another twenty minutes. I know you're curious about the park, too."

Hodgepodge stole Finn's pie crust. "We could take a brief look."

We finished eating and headed away from the busy market. Finn walked beside me, his wing feathers occasionally brushing my shoulder. I felt comfortable with him, like I'd known him longer than a few short days. He had an easy-going nature that made me feel like I didn't need to hide my pie-stained fingers from him.

"It's this way. Just past the market," he said.

"You mean Prospect Park?" I asked.

"If that's the name of the green space with the wrought iron benches."

I nodded. "It's the closest park we have around here."

"Well, your rulers are fixing it up. Take a look."

I stared with wide eyes at the dozen life-sized statues in the park. There were several ogres carrying a statue away and more being brought in.

"Who is making all of these?" I asked.

"I couldn't get an answer out of the guards," Finn said. "They basically kicked me out and told me to mind my own business. One of them said angels have no jurisdiction here and to sling my hook. He was a nice guy. I might ask him to go for a cider with me later."

"You should mind your business," Hodgepodge said. "Getting noticed by the family's royal guard will only bring trouble to your door."

"Maybe they'll make a statue of you," Finn said with a grin. "Would you like that, Hodgepodge?"

"The ones in the castle have been made in the image of people who work here," I said to Finn. "They're extraordinary. They look exactly like the real thing."

Something buzzed in Finn's pocket, and he slid it out and looked at it. "I've got to go. I'm meeting someone who has a lead on my mother. It's been great to catch up, though. We'll have to do it again. I'm around for a few weeks at least."

"We're too busy," Hodgepodge said.

"I'd like that," I said. "I'll give you my address. It's only a small place, but it's home and close to the castle."

Finn made a note of my details on the small device he pulled from his pocket. He leaned forward to kiss my cheek, but a growl from Hodgepodge made him hesitate. Instead, he touched my elbow. "It was good to see you again, Bell."

"You too."

"And you, Hodgepodge."

Hodgepodge ignored Finn.

Finn hurried away, and after a moment of watching him, I turned my attention back to the statues.

Warwick Woodsbane strode into the park, a scowl on his already surly face. Warwick was an enigma. I'd thought he was a loyal guard to the family, but his recent actions made me question who he was loyal to. He'd saved me from the castle dungeon, let me get away with snooping in the family's private rooms, and helped when we'd rescued the women from the ship. Since then, he'd fallen silent. I couldn't decide if that silence was good or not.

I discreetly waved at him, and after a few seconds, he walked toward me. There was anger in his eyes.

"Hey. What's this all about?" I asked.

"Big trouble," he muttered.

"Who's making all the statues? Did Lady Isolda commission them?"

"Not that I know of. Someone with powerful magic is creating them."

"Oh! That makes sense. There are so many."

"I have no clue who's doing it, but I don't like it," Warwick said. "Were you just talking to an angel?"

"You saw that?"

"I see everything. But those flashy wings were hard to miss. Tell your new friend to be careful. The family hates angels."

"Is there anyone they do like?" Hodgepodge asked.

"It's up for debate," Warwick said.

"I'll let Finn know to be careful," I said. "Are those statues being added to the stone chamber?"

"For now."

"If they keep being made at this rate, there won't be enough room for people to walk around."

"That's a tiny issue to worry about," Warwick said.

"Maybe for you. I'm the one cleaning them."

"I meant, the statues aren't replicas." Warwick leaned in close. "Someone is turning people into stone."

I looked around at the dozen statues, a hot horror gripping my head and making it pound. "Everyone here was once alive?"

"They still are," Warwick said. "They're trapped in stone form."

"All of them?"

He nodded, his gaze narrowing. "Is there a problem?"

"What about Augustus?" I grew lightheaded. "Someone destroyed his statue. I found it smashed and had to clear it up."

"Why is this the first time I'm hearing about this?" Warwick pivoted toward me.

"I didn't know I had to tell you! And I didn't realize it was an actual person inside the stone. If someone deliberately knocked over and destroyed Augustus..." I couldn't finish the sentence.

Warwick growled. "It means someone murdered him."

Chapter 5

"I'm still not sure we can trust Warwick." Astrid lounged on my bed, sipping from the hot cocoa I'd given her and waving her booted feet back and forth.

"He's been nothing but supportive," I said. "He wouldn't risk everything he has if he didn't mean it."

"I'm with Astrid, and I rarely agree with her." Evander was in my lodgings, too, along with Griffin. We'd gathered to discuss the stone park Finn had shown me and Warwick's revelation about the statues.

I placed a tray of almond cookies on the small table, grabbing a few for me and Hodgepodge before Astrid, Griffin, and Evander pounced.

"Warwick gained nothing by revealing magic made those statues," I said. "Or rather, magic was used to turn people into stone."

"He tricks you into trusting him," Evander said. "He softens you up before handing you to the family as a traitor."

"Warwick hates the family," I said.

"He hates some of their values," Astrid said. "That's different. He's worked for them for such a long time, I don't think he can change. Sure, he's helped us once or twice, but it's not enough to believe he's on Team Dragon."

"We're a team, now?" Griffin asked. "The last I heard, you said you were helping Bell once and that was it. Change of heart?"

"I'm at a loose end, so I don't mind sticking around for longer. Don't get used to it," Astrid said.

"I appreciate all the help I can get." I settled Hodgepodge on my lap so he wouldn't keep trying to steal people's cookies. "Whoever is using this magic to turn people into stone must have enough influence to know they can cast it without getting into trouble with the family."

"Which leaves us with two options," Evander said. "It's a member of the royal family or someone in their court they value, so they turn a blind eye to all the magically created statues."

"I vote for Lady Isolda," Astrid said. "She's the one displaying them in the chamber."

Griffin nodded. "She's always had a warped mind. When I worked for the family, I never felt comfortable around her. One wrong word, and she'd make your life miserable."

"She probably thinks the statues are cute," Hodgepodge said.

"I didn't even know such a spell existed," I said. "I was even more surprised when Warwick revealed the people are still alive and have been transformed into stone."

"Not Augustus," Griffin said. "Not now he's been destroyed. But if we can find the person who is doing this, they should be able to reverse the magic so everyone else gets out alive."

"The worst they'll have is a headache and short-term memory loss," Astrid said. "Maybe a few muscle spasms."

"Augustus isn't coming back to life, though. And you don't accidentally knock over a life-sized stone statue," Hodgepodge said, eyeing everyone's cookies. "He was killed."

"But why?" Astrid asked. "I didn't know the guy well, but he was your typical obedient assistant to the Ithric family."

"He worked for Prince Godric," I said. "When I spoke to Prince Jasper—"

"When did you have a conversation with that nasty piece of work?" Griffin asked.

"I had no choice. I'd just discovered Augustus's statue obliterated when Prince Jasper and Camilla came into the chamber. He thought I'd destroyed the statue. He told me Prince Godric's staff were working for him now. And the way he was talking, it made me think he believes Augustus is still an active member of his staff."

"He won't be thinking that by now, since Augustus hasn't shown up for work," Griffin said.

"Prince Jasper has so many assistants, I doubt he's even noted his absence," Evander said. "They surround themselves with yes people, so their deviant ways are never questioned. It's only when someone stirs trouble that they get noticed."

"What do we know about Augustus?" I asked.

"He's been around for a few years." Griffin grabbed a cookie. "He quickly rose up the ranks. His late father had something to do with foreign diplomacy. He got fired when I worked for the family."

"And Augustus was happy to continue working here?" Astrid chewed on a cookie I'd tossed her. "Why would you stay loyal to the people who ended your father's career?"

"Money. Power. Influence. Take your pick," Evander said. "Maybe he hated his old man, or he thought he could do a better job. I'm going with the money option, though."

"Augustus wasn't involved in foreign policy," Griffin said.

"Did the horses in the stables tell you that?" Evander asked, a smirk on his face.

"They make more sense than you do most days," Griffin said. "Augustus liked smoking those long pungent pipes they sell at the apothecary store. He'd come into the yard sometimes when the weather was nice and stand by the wall puffing on them as he watched me work. We talked about the horses a few times. He was more of a general assistant to Prince Godric than anything specialized."

There was a quiet tap on my door, and I opened it to find Warwick outside.

"I thought I'd drop by. Give you an update," he murmured. His gaze slid past me. "I didn't know you'd have company."

"Oh good, the double agent is here." Evander scowled at Warwick.

"Ignore him," I said. "We were discussing Augustus. We're filling in the gaps to figure out who would want him dead."

"I can help with some of that." As he stepped inside, Warwick waved away my offer of hot cocoa.

"We were also talking about whether we should trust you." Astrid rolled off the bed and strode over to Warwick. "What's in this for you?"

"I still reckon he's sweet on Bell," Evander said.

"You're too late if that's the case," Astrid said. "A charming angel has turned Bell's head. They went on their first date today."

My cheeks heated. "We did not."

"You were seen in the market. Finn bought you pie."

"Have you got spies everywhere?"

"People talk when a magnificent angel with enormous white wings strolls around the realm. Especially when he's got a pretty lady by his side." Astrid laughed as my cheeks felt like they'd caught fire.

"We were catching up," I said. "It wasn't a date."

"It definitely wasn't," Hodgepodge said. "We don't need an angel in our lives."

"Finn is just passing through. He's on a mission to find his family," I said. "Let's focus on Augustus. Warwick, what can you tell us about him?"

Warwick remained standing, his back stiff and hands loose by his side. "I had little to do with the man. He was a weasel. If he thought he could turn a profit on the information he overheard, he'd sell it on. Didn't matter to whom, so long as they paid what he demanded."

"Even family secrets?" I asked.

"He tried," Warwick said. "The trouble was, he was a dummy. He let slip some information about Prince Godric to the wrong person, and it got back to him. Augustus was hauled over the coals and threatened with time in the dungeon for his disservice. There was bad blood between those two."

"I'm amazed Prince Godric didn't fire him," Griffin said.

"It was on the cards. But before he got his marching orders, Prince Godric mysteriously vanished at sea, and Prince Jasper took over his staff." Warwick smirked before his usual surly expression slid back into place.

"If Prince Godric was still with us, I'd settle this kind of twisted behavior on his weedy shoulders," Evander said.

"You don't think..." Astrid shook her head. "No. Prince Godric is definitely dead, isn't he?"

"He's dead. We saw him get blasted with lightning magic," Griffin said. "No one could survive that."

A coiled silence slid around the room like an enchanted serpent looking for its next victim.

"We never saw his body," Evander said.

"No, there's no way he survived. I'm certain Prince Godric is dead." He'd better be. The last thing I needed was an angry prince I'd helped ruin return from his watery grave.

"He's gone," Warwick said. "I saw that blast of power annihilate him. Prince Godric always thought he was something special, but he was just an egotistical madman with access to an unhealthy amount of magic. We have nothing to worry about. Prince Godric is dead."

"I'm worried about what happened to Augustus," I said. "And I need help to look into it. There's someone out there doing this. We have to stop them."

"We do?" Evander dropped half a cookie into his mouth. "What if we discover it's Lady Isolda? You're going to take out another member of the ruling family?"

"If I have to. Although it'll be easier with your help." I looked around the group. "I know we said this would be a temporary thing, but I'm just after information."

"For now," Warwick said. "We all know what you're like. You discover disservice and want to make it right. It'll be your downfall."

"Doing the right thing should never be a person's downfall," I said. "What if more statues are destroyed?"

"None of us liked Augustus, but it sucks what happened to him," Astrid said. "I can ask around, see if anyone's heard about a dodgy spell caster with a liking for stone magic."

"For the right price, I'll ask a few questions about bodies being dredged from the sea," Evander said. "Put our minds to rest about Prince Godric."

Astrid hurled a cushion at his head. "Bell's a friend! You don't charge friends when they need help."

"I was thinking about the huge pile of darning I needed doing," Evander said. "Bell's the best."

"Don't be a jerk," Warwick said.

"I could say the same to you." Evander glowered at Warwick. "You still haven't answered the question about why you're getting involved. If word gets back to the family that you can no longer be trusted, they'll lop your head off your shoulders. There's nothing in it for you."

"It's a risk I'm prepared to take," Warwick said. "I'm doing this for Bell and the dragons. They need our help. And if there's someone powerful in the realm tinkering with stone magic, they must be stopped."

"Let's put our disagreements aside and focus on that," I said. "We'll do discrete digging and see if Augustus had enemies. Powerful ones who wanted to mess him up."

"I'll keep my ear to the ground when I'm working in the yard," Griffin said. "The other servants love to talk. Evander, are you in? No payment. Not even your darning."

"Sure, sure. I'll tap into my networks, see what I can find out," Evander said.

"I'll stay close to Prince Jasper. See if he lets anything slip about using stone magic," Warwick said.

"Perfect. When I was clearing up what was left of Augustus, I found this among the rubble. I don't know if it's useful, but it didn't respond to my cleaning spell." I pulled out the rune stone and placed it on the table.

Astrid picked it up and immediately dropped it. She wiped her hand on her tunic. "Don't you know what that is?"

Evander prodded the stone with a finger and grimaced. "If you found this with what was left of Augustus, then it was definitely murder."

"Why? What does the rune stone mean?" I asked.

"I'd like to know too," Griffin said. "It looks like a crudely drawn-on stone to me."

Warwick was inspecting the stone. "You're all being dramatic."

"What are they being dramatic about?" I asked.

"There's nothing dramatic about wanting to keep away from toxic magic." Evander's tone was light, but his expression revealed his true emotions. I'd never seen him look scared.

"The marks on the stone are based on an ancient myth," Warwick explained. "There's no solid proof to any of it."

"There's truth behind every myth," Evander said.

"Not always. Although it is strange you found the rune stone where Augustus's statue was destroyed," Warwick said.

"Fill me in. Let's assume it is real," I said. "What do those marks on the stone mean?"

Warwick sighed. "The marks represent something called the stone heart amulet. This rune stone is a calling card."

"A calling card of mockery," Astrid said. "Whoever left this is thumbing their nose and saying: *hey, look at me. I'm an all-powerful jerk, and there's nothing you can do about it.*"

I stared at Warwick, hoping he'd rebut Astrid's statement, but he nodded. "Whoever has access to the stone heart amulet is basically unstoppable."

Chapter 6

I'd barely slept last night after my friends revealed the significance of the runestone. I'd assumed it had been an offering left for the dragons and had nothing to do with Augustus's death. Although it had been odd that I'd found it scattered among his shattered remains.

Hodgepodge yawned loudly in my ear and smacked his lips together. "We need a few more hours in bed."

I stretched, poked a leg out from under the covers, and yanked it back into the warmth. "I agree. But sadly, we need to go to work and act as if everything is normal. We also need to keep an eye on Emberthorn and Stormwing. And we must catch Seraphina before we start cleaning. Her library will have more information about the stone heart amulet."

"Warwick was just showing off yesterday, talking about powerful magic."

"He's not a guy who cares what people think about him. Stay here while I get ready." I forced myself out of bed, had a quick wash, and dressed, then we were out the door.

As I hurried away from my lodgings toward the castle, Hodgepodge lazily slumped around my neck.

"It wasn't Warwick being adamant the amulet was real," I said. "Evander and Astrid were most worried. Have you ever seen Evander worry about anything?"

"Those two love to exaggerate. Lies run through their blood."

"That's untrue. Well, Evander likes to exaggerate about his success with the ladies, but Astrid is always straight with us." I nodded at the gate guards, noticing Saunders was still missing. Now I knew the reason why.

"Astrid doesn't know when she's telling a truth or a lie. Don't forget, she deceived you into going into the castle and taking a book from the family's collection. Also, she used you as her distraction while she raided the castle coffers."

"I haven't forgotten. It's just the way she is. She was raised in a family of thieves."

"Doesn't make it right," Hodgepodge said. "And it means we can't rely on her. Don't believe a word any of them tell you until you find out the facts for yourself."

"But they're our friends."

"We thought Elara was a friend, and she sold you out to the family. And what about Seraphina? If it weren't for her meddling, the dragons would never have been encased in stone," Hodgepodge said. "It's not always right to trust people at face value. Many have hidden agendas."

"Do I need to be worried about your hidden agenda?" I stepped into the cool embrace of the castle and rubbed my hands together.

"So long as there's always a supply of cookies and a cozy blanket to snuggle under with you, there'll be no agendas coming from me."

I smiled and kissed his side. "I can always rely on you. Let's see what Seraphina has to tell us."

Dawn had yet to break outside the castle, and the cold interior was still slumbering, the staff and residents tucked in their beds, not ready to start another day. However, Seraphina would be awake. She'd barely slept since Emberthorn and Stormwing roused and worked tirelessly to unpick the complicated magic that kept them contained in stone. It had been slow going, but recently, we'd made progress.

I knocked softly on her door, and a moment later, she opened it. It looked like she hadn't showered in days. Her dark clothing hung off her, and her cheeks were hollow. She gestured me in without a word then locked the door.

"If you're here to ask about the dragons, they're doing well. I crept in to see them three times last night and spent several hours with them. They're comfortable." Her voice was hoarse from exhaustion.

"I know you're doing excellent work. I trust you with them," I said. "But you must take care of yourself. If you get sick, we may not be able to complete the magic to release them."

"The hard part is done." Seraphina dismissed my concerns with a wave of her hand. "And you know what to do with the dragons. I've mixed enough potion that, if I drop dead tomorrow, you'd still be able to free them."

"Make sure you don't. I like having you around," I said.

Seraphina dropped into a chair. Dirty mugs and plates sat piled beside her. "It'll be up to you to lead them to freedom and help to negotiate a place for them. My work is almost done."

My stomach tensed at the enormity of the challenge in front of me. "One step at a time. My mother used to say, to be successful with an enormous task, you have to take Chihuahua steps. One tiny step at a time until you reach your destination."

"She was a wise woman but reckless. We can't afford to be that way. Not with so much at stake." Seraphina looked up at me with tired eyes. "I think they've forgiven me."

"I'm not sure Stormwing has," Hodgepodge said.

"Well, almost forgiven me. Stormwing is stubborn. I may have more work to do with him," Seraphina said.

I crouched in front of her and took hold of her hand. "They know how sorry you are for your betrayal. And you're making amends now. If it weren't for you, I wouldn't have the first clue how to release them from the stone. They'd be stuck. And if any member of the royal family discovered they were stirring, they'd smash them into so many pieces, no amount of glue would stick them together again. They'd take the dragon bones hidden in the statues and burn them. There'd be nothing left to resurrect."

"I know. And we're almost ready. Not long now." Seraphina closed her eyes for a second. "How's the sanctum looking?"

"Their hiding place is prepared. The roster is ready to go, and everyone is on board," I said. "Once the dragons are free, you must get some rest."

"I can manage on little sleep. I won't rest until I know they're safe."

Nothing I said to Seraphina could stop her tireless work. I patted a hand. "I'm actually here for information. Have you ever heard of the stone heart amulet?"

Her brow furrowed, and her gaze went to the enormous stacks of books all around the room. "It's an old myth. Something about a necklace imbued with the power to turn things to stone. Like a gorgon, but the magic is transferred to whoever is wearing the amulet. It's ancient. I believe the knowledge of the stone came down through oral storytelling. That means the information in any book will be distorted. Ancient whispers can't be relied upon."

"Have you got any books about it?"

"Of course. Why the interest?" Seraphina pushed herself out of the chair with some effort.

I stood and followed her. "You've noticed the new statues in the chamber?"

"They're impossible to miss." She walked slowly along the book stacks, trailing a finger against the spines and stirring tiny dust particles.

"A statue was destroyed. It was one of Prince Godric's assistants."

"I can't say I noticed. I've paid them little attention. I've been so focused on Emberthorn and Stormwing."

"I arrived to find it in pieces and had to clear it up," I said. "And I learned from Warwick that someone is using magic to turn people to stone. That's why I'm so interested in the amulet."

She stopped looking at the books and turned to stare at me. "Stone magic. Just like the dragons?"

My eyes widened. "Did you use the stone heart amulet to trap them?"

Seraphina shook her head. "No! No, that wouldn't have worked. Well, the magic would have slowed them, and it would harm them in their weakened state. I didn't think the amulet was even real, though. I assumed it was an old campfire story, grown into a scary myth." She pulled out several books and set them on a table then opened one and looked through it. "Let me check something. Stay here."

"I can get you what you need."

Seraphina ignored me and hurried off. She returned with a thick, leather-bound ledger, which she opened, checked the first page, then flipped through it. Her sigh was heavy. "It appears I was mistaken. According to this ledger, the stone heart amulet is very real. It was acquired by the family more than a decade ago."

My heart skittered. "The amulet is in the castle?"

"Which means it must be a family member using it," Hodgepodge said.

"Unless it was stolen," Seraphina said. "As you know from personal experience, things go missing from the family's collection room, no matter how closely they're guarded."

"Has there been a report of the stone heart amulet being taken?" I asked.

"Not to my knowledge, but I have been distracted. And there are few people who know how vast the family's collection of magical items is. Some of the things they keep are seriously disturbing. They use the most powerful items against those who pose the biggest threats."

"Is there any way you can check if it's still in the collection?" I asked.

"No one gets into that collection room without the family's permission," Seraphina said. "And although they give me a degree of freedom, I have no access. If I tried to get in, it would make them suspicious, and we can't afford that, not when we're so close to getting the dragons free."

"Astrid could get in," Hodgepodge said. "She's always sneaking about the castle and poking her nose into things she shouldn't."

"We'll ask her and see if she's up for the challenge," I said.

Seraphina checked another book and spent a few minutes in silent contemplation as she read the text. I opened a hefty tome with a cracked spine. It detailed how the stone heart amulet had been created in the fires of a once-active volcano using the bones of a dark witch and the essence of a goblin king. It sounded like the stuff of nightmare fairytales.

"I knew I remembered something about the amulet. It's in here. It's why so few dared to use it," Seraphina said.

I looked up at her. "There's a problem with the magic?"

"There's no good reason to turn anyone into stone. That power has a darkness that threads through it. But it's more than that. Using the amulet more than once afflicts anyone with madness. It grows worse every time they use it. The power is addictive. The more magic you cast, the more you desire it until it sends you insane."

"That sounds like the kind of thing Prince Godric would enjoy using," Hodgepodge said.

"If he was still around, I believe he's one of the few people unstable enough to use it and not fear the consequences," Seraphina said. "I doubt there is anything he wouldn't do to get the throne out from under his mother."

"Prince Godric argued with Augustus not long before he left the castle," I said. "They weren't on good terms after he tried to sell a secret about the prince."

Seraphina thumbed through more pages. "Prince Godric was not to be trusted, but Prince Jasper's no angel, either. I remember him when he was a child. There was something spiteful in his nature. He got a kick out of scaring girls and hurting his friends. He barely had any companions by the time he became a teenager because people were so wary of him. There were even rumors his parents bribed ministers' children to spend time with the prince, so he wasn't lonely. Those friendships never lasted long, no matter how big the bribe."

"He gives me the chills," Hodgepodge said. "But all members of the Ithric family do that. There's not a good one among them."

"Prince Jasper used to threaten anyone with time in the dungeons if they did something he didn't like," Seraphina said. "He has a charming exterior, but it hides a character as twisted as Prince Godric's. The only difference between them was Prince Godric didn't care who saw his dark desires."

"Prince Jasper would have access to the stone heart amulet," I said. "He could be behind this."

"Even if he is, it's too risky to question him."

"I'm staying as far away from Prince Jasper as I can, but there's no reason why we can't discreetly listen to his conversations. And I still have the potion of concealment Elara gave me."

Alarm flashed in Seraphina's eyes. "Bell, please don't sneak around listening to Prince Jasper's business. If you're caught, you'll get in serious trouble. You can't take that risk. The dragons need you."

"He has a motive for wanting Augustus dead," I said. "If Prince Jasper thought Augustus had something to do with Prince Godric vanishing, he could have gotten revenge on behalf of his brother."

"Those two hated each other," Hodgepodge said. "When I was trapped in a cage in Prince Godric's room, he throttled Jasper several times just for fun."

"They have a hate-hate relationship," Seraphina said. "Ever since they were children, they liked to see who could inflict the most pain on the other and get away with it."

"Which suggests they weren't close," I mused. "Would Prince Jasper risk his sanity for a brother he loathed?"

"I can do more research on the amulet," Seraphina said. "But everything I'm learning about it sets alarm bells jangling. You don't need to get involved. We must focus on the dragons. It's almost time to free them, and that will take all of our attention."

"As their emissary, Emberthorn and Stormwing will always be my focus," I said, "but if someone is sneaking into the castle and killing people, the dragons are at risk, too. What if someone snuck in when Emberthorn was smoking or Stormwing was grumbling and used the amulet on them?"

"The dragons are rarely on their own," Seraphina said. "When I'm not in the chamber at night, I'm resting in the servants' tunnel."

"You must have left at some point," I said. "You wouldn't have missed a stone statue being smashed on the floor."

Seraphina let out an exasperated sigh. "I take comfort breaks! But short ones. The statue's destruction must have happened just before dawn. I leave before you arrive, but there was only a period of half an hour when someone could have gotten into the chamber and destroyed Augustus's statue."

"That's all the time they needed," I said. "Whoever did this timed it perfectly. Anyone familiar with the chamber knows my working hours, and they'd have needed to arrive before dawn to ensure they didn't bump into me or the guards setting up for the day."

"I'm glad we didn't encounter them," Hodgepodge said. "They could have turned you to stone, too."

"Stay away from the stone heart amulet," Seraphina said. "You're a crucial ally of the dragons. Nothing bad can happen to you, or we won't be able to get them free."

"I'll be careful, but just because the Ithric family has influence doesn't mean they can get away with murder," I said. "If Prince Jasper is involved, he must answer for his crime."

"And I suppose you want us to make that happen?" Hodgepodge asked.

"With the resources we have, the least we can do is find out more," I said.

"I don't like this," Seraphina said, "but I recognize the look in your eyes. When you get an idea in your head, it's impossible to shake it loose."

"Don't I know it," Hodgepodge said. "Just the other week, Bell said I'd put on weight. She refused to feed me cookies for seven days! I almost perished from starvation."

I gently prodded his ample belly. "You'll never waste away."

"Let me do some digging, see if I can find out anything useful," Seraphina said. "Please, be careful."

I checked the time. "Always. We need to go. It's time to get to work."

"We focus on cleaning and keeping our heads down," Hodgepodge said.

I tickled him under the chin. "Of course. But while we do that, we can hunt for clues. And I know just where to start."

Chapter 7

"The weather isn't fit for a picnic, if that's what you're thinking." Alice handed over a wrapped parcel of dried fruit and meat. "The rain set in an hour ago, and there's no sign of it letting up."

"We're having an indoor picnic." I tucked the food inside an underskirt pocket. "I thought it would be nice to do something different on our lunch break."

"Good. Stay inside. You'll catch a chill out there." Alice glared at the rain lashing on the pane.

"Thanks, Alice. See you later." I dashed out of the kitchen with Hodgepodge and then ducked into a shadowy alcove and pulled out the potion of concealment. "What does this feel like when you take it?"

"Nothing bad. It made my skin tingle, but then I felt no different," Hodgepodge said. "But if you've reconsidered, we don't have to do this. We can eat lunch instead. This is dangerous."

"It'll be far less dangerous if we're invisible," I said. "We have to find out if Prince Jasper is involved in turning everyone to stone. If he's got his hands on the amulet, we'll all be in trouble."

"Give the potion to Evander and let him dive headfirst into danger," Hodgepodge said. "He's dumb enough to do it."

"He's not dumb, but he can be reckless. And as much as I appreciate Evander's help, he can't be trusted with something like this. He'll get distracted in Prince Jasper's chambers and be tempted to take all his shiny things. Then he'll lose focus on the mission."

"So he's the one who gets caught and in trouble," Hodgepodge said.

"We wouldn't want that to happen to a friend, would we? Three drops of this potion, and we can go anywhere in the castle. And after we've completed our quest, we'll reward ourselves with lunch before we go back to work."

Hodgepodge grumbled under his breath then opened his mouth. I placed three droplets of the potion on his tongue and then did the same, getting a hit of aniseed and something sharp. A shiver ran through me, and by the time I'd blinked, Hodgepodge had vanished.

"Can you see me?" I whispered.

"No, but I can hear you. Keep talking, so I can figure out where you are."

I spoke softly until I felt Hodgepodge climb my leg and settle on my shoulder, his invisible tail curling around my neck.

"Let's hurry and get this over with," Hodgepodge said. "I don't want my growling stomach to give us away. We should have eaten before we went on this fool's errand."

"We'll soon be eating. We don't have long." The visitors had just started a new session in the stone chamber, which gave me fifty minutes to get to Prince Jasper's private chambers and see if our prince was in residence. If he wasn't, I'd poke around his room and discover if he'd left the stone heart amulet anywhere.

Rather than risking using the main staircase to get to the private family rooms at the top of the castle, I stuck to the servants' tunnels, hurrying up the roughly cut steps until we could go no higher. I peeked out of the door.

"Stop wasting time," Hodgepodge whispered. "Trust the potion. We are invisible."

I eased open the door and stepped into the corridor. At this level, the family's showy wealth was everywhere, from the thick, lush carpet underfoot to the expensive, enormous original oil paintings of various family members on the walls, the frames tarnished gold. Small pedestal tables sat on either side of the corridor displaying vases and antiques that would most likely fund my salary for a decade.

"Go to the main staircase," Hodgepodge said. "Unless you've changed your mind. You still have time, and that food shouldn't go to waste."

"No, we're going." I checked no one would see the door open and close by itself before dashing out and tiptoeing to the bottom of the main stairs. Several of Lady Isolda's assistants were hurrying down the stairs, huddled together as they talked among themselves. I waited for them to pass then sprinted up two at a time. When I reached the top, the air was heavy with the scent of cedarwood and a faint whiff of smoke from an open hearth.

I hurried past several closed doors. Having been up here once before on a mission to rescue Hodgepodge, I knew which rooms to avoid. I sped past Prince Godric's chambers and around the corner. Prince Jasper had rooms overlooking the main castle grounds close to the west turret. I checked several rooms but found bathrooms and dressing chambers.

"I hear voices," Hodgepodge murmured.

"Prince Jasper?"

"A female voice. Possibly Camilla."

I held my breath for a few seconds and closed my eyes, tuning into the low murmurs. Something thudded on the floor, making me jump. I headed in the direction of the noise, and as I grew nearer, heard snatches of a tense conversation.

I tried the handle on a door and inched it open. Much like Prince Godric's room, there was an elegantly decorated entrance parlor with three doors leading off to different sections of Prince Jasper's private chambers. One door was open, and from a quick peek, I spotted Prince Jasper and Camilla.

"We go no further," Hodgepodge whispered. "We can listen well enough from here."

I nodded, happy to stay far away from the prince.

"You know why you're here." Prince Jasper's tone had a lyrical quality, but its playful notes didn't fool me. "Why do you have to be so stubborn?"

"I'm following protocol. It would be inappropriate to do anything else at this time." Camilla's words were so quietly spoken that I strained to hear them.

"No one else needs to know. It would show you're committed to this partnership."

"You would tell. You wouldn't be able to help yourself."

"What does that mean? You insult me. You don't think I'll be a loyal and respectful husband?"

"Do you think you will? You say you'll be respectful, but your actions tell another story," Camilla said.

"Please! A man can only wait for so long."

"The wedding is in less than a month. Surely, you won't expire in that time." From Camilla's tone, that was exactly what she wanted Prince Jasper to do.

"You're hoping I will, you cold witch. The strain of being around your waspish tongue and lack of kindness will finish me." Prince Jasper was whining, all traces of amusement gone from his voice. "Your parents said you were obedient and did everything you were told."

"I obeyed them when they offered my hand in marriage to your family," Camilla said. "I intend to make no more sacrifices until I must."

I raised my eyebrows. Camilla may be softly spoken around Prince Jasper, but she spoke her mind, and she spoke it well.

"Sacrifice! You heartless, ungrateful creature. You have everything in the palm of your hands, yet you throw away this opportunity as if it means nothing. It's not too late for us to end the agreement. Then you'd be left with only shame and disgrace. Your entire family would be ruined. I'd make sure of it."

"The same would go for your kingdom," Camilla said. "I know why I was chosen to be your bride. I've had to bear the relentless probing questions and examinations by a dozen doctors, healers, and magical mages. They all wanted to know the same thing."

"We have never hidden our realm's problem," Prince Jasper said sharply. "I believe it's merely a hiccup, but my mother is insistent this doesn't fail. She was the one who demanded the tests. I told her there was no need. None of this is my fault."

Camilla was silent for a few seconds. "Then it appears we're in the same situation, so you must understand my reluctance to entertain a romantic entanglement with you until things are official."

"Romantic entanglement! You read too many of those ridiculous novels. They put fanciful ideas into your head. This union is about creating prosperity for our families. If you refuse me, then you go against the wishes of your father and my mother." Something thudded against the wall close to the door. "I would hate to be in your position when they discover your treachery."

Hodgepodge growled softly. "He's browbeating her into submission."

"I admire her spirit. Prince Jasper is determined to get what he wants, but Camilla is having none of it," I whispered.

"I will serve my family in any way they see fit," Camilla said. "If that means becoming your wife and siring a dozen children, then that's what I'll do."

"We should get started now! Ensure we're compatible." Prince Jasper strode past the door and back again. Camilla remained motionless. "You behave like this is an ordeal. There are thousands of women who would do anything to be in your position. You'll become an Ithric princess. You'll have access to the castle's treasures, respect from the realm, and you'll ensure your family's fortunes are secured. You get everything."

"You get plenty, too," Camilla said. "Although you don't like me to, I have been speaking to my parents, and

I'm aware the deal you made changed at the last minute and is much less favorable for us."

"If you think they're backing out, don't hold your breath," Prince Jasper sneered. "They would have taken any deal. They were desperate to get you off their hands before you grew barren and even uglier than you already are."

Hodgepodge hissed softly.

"Perhaps we should put your theory to the test," Camilla said.

There was a heartbeat of silence. "What theory?"

"The thousands of women who want to be in my position. We'll host a party and invite the eligible single female members of the nobility to the castle. I'll ask each and every one of them how keen they would be to saddle themselves with you. To endure your clammy hands touching them. To have that whiskey-mired breath—"

There was a sharp slap, and Camilla gasped, her words stolen.

"I should cut that ungrateful tongue from your mouth. How dare you make fun of me." Prince Jasper was breathing so hard, it sounded like he was standing beside me.

I crept closer to the door and peered through the gap. He stood over Camilla, who held a hand against her cheek, her eyes wide with shock.

"You don't scare me," she said, although her words shook. "I've met plenty of bullies. Every royal court has them. Before you strike me again, imagine how it will look on our next public tour when I explain the handprint on my face was given to me by my beloved fiancé. I doubt your mother would be pleased with your progress. She may decide to exile you to the swamp lands. And I'd encourage her if she did."

Prince Jasper grabbed Camilla by the shoulders and shook her.

A gasp flew from my lips before I could stop it, and Camilla's gaze darted to the door. I backed away. "She didn't see us, did she? Are we still invisible?"

"She didn't see us, but she heard you! Get us out of here," Hodgepodge said.

"What's the matter with you now?" Prince Jasper asked.

"I thought I saw something," Camilla said. "In the entryway."

"It's just us. No one would dare enter without my permission. Stop being hysterical."

I looked over my shoulder. Camilla had wriggled out of Prince Jasper's grasp and was hurrying toward the door. She was still staring at me. I took a risk, pulled open the door leading into the corridor, and dashed out. I ran past the oil paintings and expensive vases toward the main staircase, trying to be silent, but it was impossible to run on tiptoes.

A few seconds later, Camilla blasted out of the door and followed us.

"She can see us! We should hide," I whisper-hissed to Hodgepodge.

"I'm telling you, she can't! Keep going. She's most likely hearing things. Your footsteps aren't silent."

I ducked into a room, the door standing open, and hid behind it, pressing my back against the wall and covering my mouth to stifle any sound.

Camilla rushed past, heading toward the staircase.

I let out a quiet breath. We were safe. The magic hadn't failed. It was my panic that had let us down. I crept out from behind the door and watched her progress. After a few moments of looking around, Camilla slowly retreated, heading back to Prince Jasper's chambers. Her head was down, her shoulders slumped.

"Please, if anyone is there, help me. I'm all alone with these monsters," she whispered.

My fingernails dug into the wooden doorframe. Camilla sounded heartbroken and alone, but she was practically a part of the family. I couldn't trust her. And I couldn't help her.

We waited until a door closed and then waited a minute more. I peeked into the corridor. It was empty. I dashed down the stairs, heading to the servants' tunnels, and shook off the invisibility potion.

Hodgepodge also popped into view. "That was close. You almost got us slung in the dungeon."

"I'm not used to using magic. I didn't think the potion was working." I hurried back to the stone chamber.

Hodgepodge gave my neck a gentle squeeze with his tail. "It's not your fault, lassie. We've been too long without what comes naturally to us. Hopefully, that's about to change. Let's not waste our time chasing this quest to find the stone heart amulet. We focus on the dragons."

"But we saw Prince Jasper's true nature," I said. "His charming smile is a front. I almost preferred it when Prince Godric was around. At least he didn't hide how nasty he was."

"They're as nasty as they come. Stay clear."

I checked there were no visitors in the chamber then hurried inside to clean. I stopped dead. Two new statues had appeared.

"Whoever is using the amulet isn't slowing down." I peered into the faces of the recent arrivals. "I don't recognize these two."

"Good thing too, since there are people trapped in there. We don't want to lose anyone we care about."

"Hey! I hope you don't mind me interrupting."

I turned on my heel, surprised to see Finn striding across the chamber, looking even more handsome than our last encounter, although I couldn't imagine how he'd achieved that, since he was already stunning.

"Of course not. I have to work, though." I glanced at the closed door. "How did you get in?"

"I used my charm and a little bribery money." He smiled at us. "I wanted to see if you were free later, so we could catch up."

"I finish at midnight, if that's not too late for you."

"That sounds good. Late supper it is," Finn said. "I won't keep you. I see the visitors left quite a mess for you to sort through."

I pointed at Emberthorn, who was surrounded by gifts of food, drink, flowers, and small amounts of money. "Even though we don't have any dragons striding around, people still love to see them."

Finn inspected the dragons. "They're incredible. Huh! If I narrow my eyes, it looks like they're moving."

I choked out a laugh. That was a story for another time. A story I wasn't quite ready to tell.

Finn turned back to me. "I'll stop by at midnight, and we can figure out supper together."

"Looking forward to it." I smiled as I watched him go.

"Don't get all googly-eyed over the angel," Hodgepodge grumbled. "No good will come of it."

"It's just supper with a new friend."

"The way you're grinning and skipping around, you think of him as much more than a friend."

I laughed to myself. It had been a long time since I'd considered a relationship, but maybe that was because I was waiting for the right person. Was Finn that person?

Cleaning and waiting filled the rest of the afternoon and evening. The hours dragged by as I eagerly anticipated my late supper with Finn. It was ridiculous. I was in my middle years and, as Hodgepodge said, going googly-eyed over an angel I barely knew wasn't appropriate. If I'd been eighteen, perhaps. But in your forties, weren't you supposed to have everything figured out?

I was doing a final circuit of the chamber, checking the dragons were comfortable and making sure I hadn't missed any rubbish, when the back door into the chamber smashed open. Camilla stumbled in and collapsed on the stone floor with a groan.

Chapter 8

I gestured at Hodgepodge to hide. I couldn't risk Camilla rousing and reporting back to Prince Jasper that there was a small dragon on the loose in the castle.

"Let's go," he whispered as he concealed himself behind Emberthorn's substantial bulk.

"We can't leave her. She's unconscious!" I tiptoed closer to Camilla, who was face down on the floor.

"It's a trap."

"Why would Camilla want to trap us?"

"Don't be so naïve. She may not be married to Prince Jasper yet, but she's still a member of this family. Her loyalty is to them."

"I'll make sure she's not hurt, then we'll leave."

Hodgepodge muttered to himself but stayed out of sight as I approached Camilla. I tentatively touched her shoulder. She didn't move.

I couldn't see any injuries, but the way she'd raced in here suggested all wasn't well. I gently turned her over. Her cheeks were flushed, and her lashes were wet with tears. The mark on her face from where Prince Jasper had struck her almost glowed. Then I saw bruise marks on one wrist and scowled. Prince Jasper was mistreating her. And it would only get worse. No wonder she'd run.

I grabbed my mug of water and returned to her side, gently dabbing her cheeks with a damp, clean cloth. She murmured something under her breath, and her eyes flickered open. For a second, she seemed confused. Then she jerked upright, almost head-butting me.

"Careful! I think you fainted," I said.

"Who... who are you? Where am I?" Her skittish gaze flashed from me to the chamber and back again.

"I'm Bell Blackthorn. You ran into the stone chamber a few moments ago. I was checking to see if you were injured."

She brushed away my hand, which hovered close to her cheek. "I don't remember that. Are you sure?"

"Um... yes. This is a safe place. I was about to close the doors for the night. There won't be any more visitors coming in if you need a minute to recover."

Camilla's gaze flicked around the chamber once more. "I know this place. I wanted to visit when I first arrived. It sounded so exciting."

"I remember. Everyone was looking forward to you joining the household." I remained crouched beside Camilla as her composure slipped back into place and the scared woman vanished. "Would you like something to drink?"

Camilla shook her head. "I don't want anyone to see me like this. Well, no one else."

"Give me a minute, and I'll lock the doors. As I said, all the visitors have gone, so it'll only be the castle patrols coming in here."

"No! No one! I won't allow anyone to see me in such a state of disarray. It's unbecoming."

"Of course. I'll be back in a moment." I dashed to the door Camilla had come through, closed it, and bolted it from the inside. I was supposed to leave the doors unlocked so the guards could patrol, but I'd make sure one of the doors was unbolted before leaving. I hurried to the other door and slid the bolt into place, too. By the time I returned to Camilla, she had gotten to her feet, smoothing down her crumpled silk gown. "Would you like me to accompany you back to your room?"

"I'm going nowhere. Not for now." She glanced at me again. "What did you say your name was?"

"Bell. I clean the stone chamber."

"Alone?"

"I sometimes have help. They've yet to replace the woman who used to work with me, though. She... decided not to return to her duties after a stressful time in her life."

"I imagine the drudgery of cleaning is stressful," Camilla said. "Although you get to spend time with these beautiful dragons. That's a consolation."

Surreptitiously, I blocked her view of Stormwing as best I could. He'd been restless and grumpy all day, and the last thing he'd appreciate was a sulky-faced bride-to-be poking at him. I couldn't guarantee he wouldn't bite her head off if she got too close.

"Is there anything I can do to help you?" I asked. "When you came in, it looked like you were running from someone."

"There's nothing you can do." Camilla stared at the statues. "There are so many new additions. These weren't here when I was shown around. Where are they coming from?"

"Lady Isolda has been bringing them in. Their origins are an oddity."

"Not to her. She must know where she's getting them. But why people and not dragons?" Camilla's voice no longer shook as her demure façade settled into place.

"Smaller and quicker to make than giant dragons, I suppose." Although that question had me wondering if the stone heart amulet had limitations. Maybe it couldn't turn anything larger than a person into stone.

"I wonder if there's one of me," Camilla said.

"I can guarantee there isn't."

She shot me a glance. "Is that so? You have the ear of Lady Isolda, do you? You tell her what statues to commission?"

"No! I didn't mean that. I meant... I'm certain you're not here. I clean the statues daily, and I'd recognize one of you."

"What about my husband-to-be? Has someone immortalized Jasper into stone?" Camilla headed to the edge of the chamber, and I was grateful she did so because it took her away from the dragons. "If there is one of Jasper, I intend to deface it."

I bit my bottom lip to hide a smile. "He's not here, either."

"More's the pity."

I followed a few steps behind her. "You're unhappy with Prince Jasper?"

"That's none of your concern." Camilla stopped in front of the statue of Saunders, the gate guard. "This is not what I expected."

"It's an excellent likeness."

"Not the statue. This! The castle. Royal life. The dreadful Ithric family. Is it always like this?" She turned and stared at me, her expression stark.

"I'm... unsure what you mean."

"I knew there would be duties to perform, and I was looking forward to it. I want to be part of the realm and have subjects who respect and admire me. But when I've been out in public with Jasper, there's an unpleasant mood. People are unhappy. They carefully stage everything, but the discontent is clear. People don't like the royal family, do they?"

There was no way I was sharing my true thoughts about the Ithric family. "I really couldn't say."

"You can, and you should. I need to know what I'm getting myself into." Camilla settled her hands on her hips, her glare fierce. "I knew this wouldn't be a love match, but I hoped I'd at least like Jasper. What do you think of him?"

I maintained my composure, trying not to sweat. "I don't know any member of the royal family. I work for them."

"Speak freely in front of me. I have no fondness for Jasper or anyone else in the Ithric family. They have shown me no kindness since I've arrived, and they cheated my family on the deal. I accepted I was a commodity to be exchanged, but at the last second, Lady Isolda imposed stiff taxes on my family when using local shipping routes." Camilla gave a delicate snort. "We'll be getting half of what we expected in the original deal, yet I'm supposed to perform my duty with Jasper and provide him with dozens of children."

My eyebrows flashed up. "Dozens!"

She waved a hand in the air. "Enough so the family reign will continue. What do they say, an heir and a spare? Jasper is talking about six, at least. I suppose I'll have staff to deal with all the children. But it's wrong! I should provide him with two at the most and then shut shop."

"I... I hear he has a temper." My gaze went to the bruises on her wrist.

Camilla tugged down her sleeve to conceal the marks. "When we first met, I was charmed. He was funny and sweet, and I was cautiously optimistic we could make things work. But then I arrived here, and everything changed. This castle is joyless. And so dreary and cold. Like its heart has been torn out and stamped on."

"I'm sorry you think that. When we had better weather, it could be beautiful. With the dragons gone, the climate isn't stable."

"It quickly became apparent Jasper only wanted my family's money and my fertility." Camilla continued speaking as if she hadn't heard me. "He cares nothing for me. His kindness was a veneer that cracked when he got me here."

"That's unfortunate."

Camilla threw up her hands. "I want a fairytale romance. I thought by marrying a prince and moving into his grand castle, I'd get everything I desired. But it's the opposite. It's cold and indifferent, and everywhere I go, people are scared. Are you scared of the royal family?"

"It's been a trying time since we lost our dragons," I said. "The realm has suffered. But the family is hoping to make things right with your marriage to Prince Jasper."

"They pin their hopes on a fantasy." Camilla turned and walked away, inspecting the statues again. "I should have known there'd be nothing good about a realm that can't even keep their dragons alive."

I nodded as I followed her. "Do you have to marry Prince Jasper?"

Camilla kept her back to me. "My family demands it. They need the shipping routes that run through this territory to expand. I accept I'm more of a valuable commodity to them than a daughter."

"Even so, that can't be easy," I said.

She glanced at me. "You're fortunate that no one sees value in you, so you'll never be traded or sold to the highest bidder. And at your age, I suppose you're practically invisible. Lucky thing."

I pressed my lips together and scowled at her back. "I thank the dragons every day."

"I wish we could swap places. I could spend my time here with the statues, and you'd have to deal with Jasper and his unkind words and clammy hands. I've never met a man with such damp hands. He's like the human version of a slug."

I couldn't stop the laugh that slipped out and immediately put a hand up to mask it.

Camilla turned to me again, and this time she was smiling. "Please, don't hide your laughter. It's such a rare sound in this castle. All I hear are the footsteps of marching guards ensuring order and the brusque bite of

Lady Isolda's words. It's tedious and tiring. Does no one have any fun around here?"

"Sometimes. There are nice places in the village. And there's a beautiful woodland not far away. I sometimes go walking on my day off."

Camilla looked down at her silky robe. "I'm not one for walking. My family discourages all forms of exercise. It's bad for the heart."

"Then I'm done for, since I'm on my feet all day."

"It shows."

My tongue refused to remain still. "I could outrun an ogre if I had to."

Camilla's eyes widened, and she blinked several times. "Why would you need to do that?"

"Just looking at the positive in this situation."

"I suppose when you have so little, you need to find all scraps of joy."

I was glad Hodgepodge was hiding because he'd have plenty of harsh Scottish curse words to toss at Camilla for her insults.

"What magic do you use to keep this place so spotless?" she asked. "I suppose it's your specialty."

"No magic. There are few people permitted to use any spells, potions, or magical items."

"Oh! I forget. Where I'm from, there are much fewer restrictions on magic. You never use magic?"

"I occasionally use a cleaning spell if I'm in a hurry or the visitors have been excitable and made a mess."

Camilla settled herself on the base of a stone statue and looked up at me. "That must be hard. We all have this dragon-given gift. I don't use magic a lot, but I enjoy the power on my fingertips. When I don't use it for a few days, I get an itch at the back of my neck, and I know it's my power building. Do you ever feel that?"

I hesitated. Was Camilla fishing for information to give to the family? If I said I longed to use my magic, would I get in trouble?

"Bell, you have nothing to fear from me. I may be marrying into this family, but I'm not one of them. And if I have any power and influence as a princess, I'll see if I can change things. Maybe Lady Isolda will soften when she has a few grandchildren and can relax her stranglehold on people's magic. It's not wrong to want to use it."

Camilla sounded genuine, but I was still cautious. "I would like to use it more than I do. It feels good to cast spells. And as you can see from the ceiling height, it would be impossible for me to clean that high without a little boost."

"There you go. Magic is for all of us."

"Have you told Prince Jasper that?"

Her relaxed demeanor changed, and her shoulders stiffened. "He never listens. When we became a couple, he would sit and talk to me. We discussed everything from politics to hobbies. I can't believe I was so badly fooled. Still, like you, I need to make the best of a dreadful situation."

"I hope you find a solution that brings you happiness," I said.

"Camilla! Where is my darling fiancée? We have business to finish." Prince Jasper's slurred words sounded close to the locked chamber door.

Camilla was already on her feet and dashing to the opposite door. "I do not want to be anywhere near him."

I hurried after her and unbolted the door. "If you turn left, you'll come across the main staircase. Can you find your way back to the family level?"

"Yes! I'll find a room to hide in until Jasper sobers up. He's mildly less repugnant when he's not drunk out of his gourd." Camilla turned back to me and grabbed my hand. "Thank you, Bell." She dashed away.

A second later, Hodgepodge landed on my shoulder with a grunt. "Prince Jasper is outside the other door. It's time for us to flee, too."

"What about the dragons?"

"I checked them while you were dealing with Camilla. They're comfortable and sleeping. Seraphina will be by soon to check on them. We must get out of here."

I nodded just as Prince Jasper thudded on the closed door at the opposite end of the chamber. I grabbed my cleaning things, ran out of the door, and eased it shut. I turned and face-planted into a broad chest that smelled of spun sugar. I staggered back and looked up into Finn's dazzling smile.

"There you are," he said. "Is everything okay? I was worried you'd changed your mind about supper. I went to your place, but you weren't there."

"No! Sorry, I got delayed."

"Are you free now?"

"Free and eager to get out of here." I glanced at the closed door.

"Then let's have our date, shall we?"

Chapter 9

"Remember what I said," Hodgepodge whispered into my ear as we walked alongside Finn and away from the stone chamber. "He's not to be trusted."

I couldn't reply without Finn overhearing, so I shook my head. "Did you make progress in locating your mother?"

"No, my source was a dead end. We were talking about two different people. At first, I thought I was onto something, but she's like the invisible woman," Finn said.

"I know how that feels," I said. "Sometimes, invisibility can be a useful trait."

Finn looked down at me. "I can't imagine anyone passing you without noticing."

My cheeks heated, and my stomach did a flip of happiness. I'd not felt that for a long time. "What would you like for supper?"

Finn pointed at the bag he carried. "I brought a feast. I went around the market after I finished my meeting and chose a few goodies. I didn't know what you like, so I got a selection."

"That sounds great."

"I'm not hungry," Hodgepodge said.

"Do you like fresh apricots?" Finn asked, a playful grin on his lips.

"No."

"He loves apricots," I said. "All fruit, actually. And dried meat. All desserts, especially pie. Actually, there's not much Hodgie won't eat."

"Then Hodgepodge is in for a treat. I got the last of the pie from that stall we went to. Apple and blackberry."

"That sounds delicious," I said.

I glanced over my shoulder as we exited the castle. I was happy to see Prince Jasper wasn't following. I was worried about Camilla, though. If he found her, the result wouldn't be pretty.

"Is something on your mind?" Finn asked.

"It's been a busy day."

"If you have a mystery to solve, I'm happy to help," he said.

"You'll be no help to us, laddie," Hodgepodge said.

"I've solved a few crimes while working at Angel Force. Or I'm happy to listen while you talk through any dilemma you're facing. No judgment from me. You wouldn't believe some of the crazy cases I've had to solve."

"With Juno and Zandra's help, no doubt," Hodgepodge said.

"Sure. Life has become more interesting since they moved to Crimson Cove. Juno has a knack for pulling together the puzzle pieces and figuring out what happened."

Juno was a magical talking familiar we'd encountered when she'd been solving a tricky murder with her witch companion. She was a smart, stunning white cat with a hint of something special about her. She made an excellent ally, but I wouldn't want to get on her wrong side.

"That's who we need here, not you," Hodgepodge said to Finn.

"Hodgepodge! Finn is our guest. Be nice."

"It's fine. I understand Hodgepodge is being protective of you. And I'm glad he is. You need supporters on your side, especially if you have a lot on your plate," Finn said.

My opinion of Finn warmed, and it was already on pleasant terms. Hodgepodge was being downright rude, but Finn was taking it in his stride.

"What do you think of the village?" I asked.

"It's cute. Quaint. But it's strange to walk around and see barely any magic being used. And there's this atmosphere, as if something is about to blow. Does that make sense?"

"Complete sense," I said. "There have been grumblings for a while since magic use was restricted. And with the dragons gone, people are struggling."

"For a while, by the looks of it," Finn said. "I flew out as far as I could and ended up in a dismal gray swampland. I talked to a few of the locals, and they had nothing good to say about your ruling family."

I nodded. "From what I've learned recently, the Ithric family ignores the outer realm towns and villages."

"That can't be good for business," Finn said. "In the end, they'll have to take care of everyone, or they'll wind up with a rioting group of troublemakers who've stirred themselves into a frenzy."

"It's already happening," I said. "The family is pinning their hopes on the upcoming royal wedding. But the way things are going, there may not be one."

"Is that so?"

I shrugged. "If you believe the gossip."

"Gossip can be useful to gain insider information."

We reached my lodgings and walked inside. Finn had to tuck his wings close to his back to get through the door and then stood for a moment, inspecting the place. "This is cozy. Shall I bank the fire?"

"Thanks. Heating is a luxury around here, and it's yet to reach the servants' quarters."

Finn placed the food on the kitchen counter then crouched beside the fire. He rubbed his hands together, and a flame shot out from his palm and sparked to life among the prepared kindling.

"Neat trick," I said.

He rolled his shoulders as he stood. "It's one of the few benefits of being part demon. I run hot."

"Mind you keep your demon under wraps when you're around Bell," Hodgepodge said, still glued to my shoulder, his red leathery ruff flared in a show of anger.

"He's behaving himself," Finn said. "Although I went through a time when it wasn't easy to control him."

"Sounds dangerous," Hodgepodge said. "How many times a day does your demon side come out and cause destruction?"

Finn grimaced. "It's getting less frequent. And I always have friends around to help me if he becomes a problem."

I busied myself by unloading the food. "In case he becomes a problem while you're here, what should we do?"

"Juno normally bites or scratches me. She also hisses in my face. Sometimes, Zandra has to whack me on the butt with a painful spell. Basically, any form of pain snaps me back."

"I'll be happy to inflict pain on you." Hodgepodge slid off my shoulder and dropped onto the kitchen counter as I took the pie out of its box.

"All of this food looks amazing," I said.

"I haven't gone overboard?" Finn asked. "I figured since you were working all day, you'd be hungry."

"Starving. Thanks." I spent a few minutes fixing plates of food for us, and even though Hodgepodge said he wasn't hungry, he carefully directed me to exactly how much pie he wanted and how many apricots he needed sliced and their stones removed.

Once we were settled in seats around the fire, we enjoyed our plates of food in a comfortable silence.

"So, what's got you so busy?" Finn asked.

"It's none of your business," Hodgepodge said.

Finn arched an eyebrow. "How's the pie?"

Hodgepodge's mouth was so full he couldn't answer, so he simply grunted.

"Glad you're enjoying it." Finn smiled at me. "You can trust me. We don't know each other well, but I have nothing to gain from airing your problems to strangers."

The more time I spent with Finn, the more I trusted him. I finished my mouthful of pie and spent a few minutes filling him in on the surprise arrival of the stone statues, Augustus's murder, the discovery of the rune stone, and my concerns there was an out-of-control, dangerous magic user causing trouble.

Finn sat back and blew out a breath. "Wow! No wonder you're so stressed and busy."

"It's not my typical day in the castle," I said. "In your work at Angel Force, have you ever come across anything called the stone heart amulet? It seems to be behind our troubles."

He shook his head. "It doesn't ring any bells."

"Someone has it, and the more they use it, the more dangerous they become," I said. "If we can identify the person who has the amulet, we can reverse the magic and save everyone else."

"But not Augustus, since he was knocked over and destroyed?" Finn asked.

"It's too late for him," I said.

"Do you know who might have wanted him dead?" Finn asked. "You need to gather a list of suspects."

"We're not investigators," Hodgepodge said.

"No, but we have a network of connections," I said. "And we've already got people asking around about Augustus. I tried to get into Prince Jasper's chambers to see if he's involved, but I didn't get far."

Finn set down his plate. "Weren't you worried about getting caught?"

"I told Bell not to do it," Hodgepodge said. "And we were almost discovered."

"From what I'm learning about your royal family, and I have been doing digging of my own," Finn said, "they're not people you mess around with and expect to survive to tell the tale."

I swallowed the fear that simmered inside me. "I'm concerned a family member is involved in Augustus's murder. The family has a vast collection room containing a horde of magical items, and they had the stone heart amulet in their private collection. Now, someone's got it and is misusing it. It makes sense it would be a family member, since they had the easiest access to it."

Finn nodded along as I talked. "I read a lot about Lady Isolda being the family powerhouse. She has two sons, too, doesn't she?"

"Technically, she has two sons," I said. "Prince Godric's not around. Everyone's grateful for that."

"Where's he gone?"

I half-smiled. "Are you ready to hear another long and involved story?"

He grinned. "Definitely."

"I'll make hot cocoa before I begin."

Fifteen minutes later, Finn was up-to-date with the disappearing women, Prince Godric's involvement, and dragon blood sacrifices. By the time I'd finished, he was staring at me openmouthed.

"Bell! Have you got some kind of magical superpower I don't know about?"

"Invisibility? Well, not really invisibility magic, but people rarely notice me. It helps me listen in to conversations and see things others may not want me to see. And it helped that Prince Godric was getting desperate and making mistakes. I was just around to put the pieces together and make sure he didn't hurt anyone else."

"Are you sure he's dead?" Finn asked.

"He couldn't have survived the blast of magic that hit him."

"All the stone statues showing up sounds like the kind of crazy thing he'd do," Finn said.

"I told Bell she shouldn't get involved in this muddle." Hodgepodge was on his back, his distended belly exposed for me to scratch. "She won't stop nosing about, though. It'll get her killed."

I gathered Hodgepodge in for a hug and kissed his head. "That's not possible while you're looking after me."

"I'm glad you have Hodgepodge by your side," Finn said. "But... no offence. He's small. Are you sure you've got enough backup to deal with this dubious family?"

Hodgepodge growled at Finn, and I chuckled. "Don't worry. Hodgepodge has a unique set of skills."

There was a tap on the front door, and before I'd risen from my seat to open it, Astrid strode in. She stopped dead when she saw I had company. Then a sly smile crossed her face. "So, you two finally hooked up."

"They're not hooking up," Hodgepodge said. "I'm here to make sure nothing untoward happens."

I introduced Finn and Astrid to each other. "We were talking over what's going on with the statues."

"We'll get to that in a minute." Astrid unhooked a blade from the belt slung low around her hips and strode to Finn, straddled him, pressing the blade against his neck.

"Astrid!" I jumped up.

"What are you doing here?" she asked Finn.

"Looking into my family," he said calmly.

"How did you first meet Bell?"

"Astrid, that's enough," I said. "Finn's a friend."

Astrid ignored me. "Answer my question. Are you after Bell for something?"

Finn slid a glance my way. "Her friendship."

"How did you meet?"

"Hodgepodge was injured and ended up in my sanctuary in Crimson Cove. Bell felt she owed me a favor and helped with an investigation. Well, helped me and some friends." Finn's calm gaze remained on Astrid.

"That's right," I said. "Now, get off him and remove the blade from his throat!"

Astrid pressed the blade even closer. "What intentions do you have toward my friend?"

"I... I like her." Finn glanced at me again. "I thought it would be fun to hang out with a new friend."

"And?"

"And nothing! If you don't get off him this second, you're no longer welcome here," I said.

Astrid drew a breath, her glare still pinned to Finn. "Be kind to Bell. She doesn't have a bad bone in her body, but she's way too trusting. She's always looking to help the underdog. Don't pull the pity card on her and get her in trouble by making her owe you more favors."

"There's no trouble to get into, and Finn would never do that to me." I grabbed Astrid's elbow. "Get off him this second."

Astrid grinned as she flicked the blade back into its sheath. "Just needed the angel to know I'm watching him."

"Not like that, you don't." I finally pulled her away from Finn. "And just so you know, I can look after myself. And I'm not naïve nor too trusting. You make me sound pathetic."

Hodgepodge grumbled several times. "You can be a little too trusting. Do I need to remind you about Camilla's fainting act and you two ladies sharing secrets over the statues?"

"What's this about the royal brood mare?" Astrid asked.

I shook my head. "That was nothing."

Astrid arched a brow. "Spill. You're rubbing shoulders with the fancy types these days?"

"Camilla was upset with Prince Jasper and needed help. No one would have abandoned her in that situation. Not even you," I said.

"I would," Astrid said. "We can't trust that one. Anyway, I'm not here to grill your boyfriend or talk about the princess in waiting and how many delightful children she won't have with Prince Jasper. I have information about Augustus."

Chapter 10

Once I was satisfied Astrid wouldn't interrogate Finn anymore and was settled with her own mug of hot cocoa and some cookies, I eagerly waited for her update about Augustus.

She ate four cookies before she felt ready to talk. "Augustus was dating a witch."

"Is that a problem?" Finn asked. "Does your royal family exclude witches?"

"No. There are plenty of witches still around. But the powerful ones keep to themselves and stay away from the Ithric family. Know where to look in the forest, and the place is full of them."

"This witch is something special." Astrid thumped her empty mug on the small coffee table. "Sabine Charming. Have you ever heard of her?"

I shook my head. "If she lives around here, our paths haven't crossed."

"She has a place tucked away deep in the woods. And until recently, she was seeing Augustus behind his wife's back."

"There's a motive there," Finn said. "Augustus stopped seeing Sabine, so she decided no one else could have him."

"Or the wife could be involved," Hodgepodge said. "A scorned, suspicious wife decided she'd had enough of her cheating hubby, so she stole the amulet and turned him to stone."

"I'm surprised Augustus was dating a witch, given his privileged position," I said. "If Prince Godric learned of their connection, he wouldn't have been impressed."

"Augustus must have liked playing on the dark side," Astrid said. "He was a prominent member of the Royal Court, which made him arrogant. Arrogance equals carelessness. He probably figured no one would track his movements and catch him messing about with someone he shouldn't."

"How did you learn of their relationship?" Finn asked.

"Villagers love to gossip. People saw Augustus slinking off to the woods."

"Have you spoken to Sabine?" I asked.

"She's almost impossible to find if she doesn't want to be," Astrid said. "I've got her general location, though, and looked around the Mistborn Moors. There's powerful magic in those moors, but no matter what I did to bring it down, it wouldn't reveal what it was hiding. Get through that magic, and I reckon you'll find Sabine. Whether she'll give us answers is another challenge to get through."

"If a powerful witch doesn't want to be found, we're out of luck," Hodgepodge said. "It's best we stay away from her. We'll remain comfy at home and eat more cookies."

"We can't ignore Sabine if she's a suspect in this investigation," I said.

"You're leading on this investigation, are you?" Astrid quirked an eyebrow. "I thought Hodgepodge told you to be more careful after your close encounter with death."

"I've just been hearing about those close encounters," Finn said.

"And do you approve?" Astrid asked. "Or are you the kind of jerk who keeps his woman under control and doesn't let her do her own thing?"

"Bell doesn't need my permission to do anything," Finn said. "But naturally, I'm concerned about her welfare. And as a friend, I'm sure you are, too."

Astrid grunted. "Whatever you say, fly boy. Anyway, I asked around, found out about the secret witch girlfriend, but that's where I hit a dead end. If Sabine doesn't want company, there's nothing we can do to convince her to talk."

"I'll try," I said. "I can go tomorrow during a break. There's a portal tunnel that goes right to the moors. I could be there and back in an hour. No one would notice me going for a walk."

"What makes you think Sabine will talk to you?" Astrid asked.

"Because Bell is nice to everyone," Hodgepodge said. "She never has a hidden agenda."

Astrid shrugged. "Neither do I."

Hodgepodge flared the leathery ruff around his neck. "You didn't mislead Bell into breaking into the castle and stealing a book while you plundered the family's fortune?"

Astrid's chuckle had an awkward edge. "I forget. Something like that may have happened, but Bell was never in any danger."

"That's all in the past," I said. "This is progress. We now have two suspects in Augustus's murder. The angry, jilted girlfriend and the cheated-on wife. What do we know about his wife?"

"Nothing yet. Still working on it," Astrid said.

"How do you want to handle this?" Finn asked.

"Don't go poking your nose where it's not wanted," Astrid said. "Bell knows what she's doing."

Hodgepodge lifted a foot, and Astrid high-fived it.

"I wouldn't dream of it, but the offer of help is there if you want it, Bell. I've no need to rush back to Crimson Cove if you need backup."

"Bell has all the backup she requires," Astrid said. "You sticking around with your flashy smile and big wings distracts her and draws attention to us."

"That's what I keep saying," Hodgepodge said, "but no one listens to me."

"I'm listening, but I'll decide if I'm getting distracted." I didn't look at Finn. "We'll go to the moors tomorrow and find Sabine."

"What do you think?" I brushed the last of the dirt away as I dashed around Emberthorn. It was midday, and we'd had a busy morning in the stone chamber as visitors bustled in and out, leaving their offerings for the dragons and studying the new additions.

"I don't dismiss the idea a powerful witch could be behind this," Emberthorn's low tone grumbled, "but the statues smell of primal power. I'm convinced dragon magic is involved in their creation. It's hot magic. Old magic."

"How can a dragon be involved?" I stowed away my cleaning equipment in various buckets and stood in front of him. "There are no active dragons in the realm. If any were flying around, they'd be spotted and brought down by the family. I still think we're onto something with the stone heart amulet."

"The rune stone you found among Augustus's remains is troubling. But that amulet needs an activator. An immensely strong magic user to steer it. Someone unafraid to blast out power and have no fear of the consequences."

My brow furrowed. "Which leads us back to the Ithric family. They're the only ones in the entire realm who can freely use any magic they desire and not be held accountable."

"What about the forest witch?" Emberthorn asked. "From your description, Sabine Charming must have power, especially if she can hide from the family."

"It's a theory I'm pursuing. Once the next visitor session starts, I'm heading to the moors with Hodgepodge."

"Be careful, Bell," Emberthorn said. "Moor witches are creatures of nature, not dissimilar to dragons. They can be impulsive and have a strong dislike for outsiders."

"I'll tread carefully," I said. "She may not even reveal herself to us."

"I'm hoping that's the option that plays out," Hodgepodge said. "We don't need some angry witch blasting magic at us."

"Once we explain what's going on, she'll want to help," I said. "Unless she's guilty, and then we'll need to run as fast as we can."

"Dragon speed to you both," Emberthorn said.

A guard looked into the room, and I gave him a thumbs-up to let him know we were ready for visitors, then dashed to the servants' tunnels. I stashed my cleaning equipment, grabbed my cloak, and headed into the cool early afternoon.

My rapid footsteps took me toward the portal tunnel, but before I could reach the plain lump of rock, someone called my name. Hodgepodge tensed on my shoulder then slid down my body and concealed himself in the large pocket in my underskirt, pressing himself almost flat so the ruched fabric concealed him.

Camilla hurried toward me, ignoring the curious glances from the people she passed. "Bell! I'm so happy to see you. I was planning on coming by the chamber. Where are you off to with such purpose?"

"Oh! Nowhere special. I'm on my lunch break. How about you?" I had no time for Camilla and couldn't afford any delays in my visit to Sabine.

"I don't have a lunch break, silly. It's not as if the family put me to work. Well, not yet, anyway." The tears were gone, the mark on her cheek barely visible, and Camilla's smile looked almost genuine.

I bobbed my head, my cheeks flushing. "Of course not. Is there something I can help you with?"

"Lots of things." Camilla stepped closer and caught hold of my elbow. "I wanted to thank you. You saw me at a low moment when I arrived in the dragon chamber, and you were nothing but kind."

"Think nothing of it. I couldn't leave you when you were upset."

"It's a lot more than most people would do. I've cried plenty of times in front of Jasper, and he laughs and tells me to pull myself together as if I'm a child! He's a beast."

"Perhaps he's not used to dealing with someone so in touch with her emotions," I said. "Lady Isolda always maintains a steely composed demeanor."

"He is used to getting his own way with just about everything, and he hates it when someone stands up to him and his brattish ways." Camilla tucked a hand into my elbow. "Walk with me, and we shall gossip. Are you sure you're not off on an adventure? You looked like you were planning on using the portal tunnel."

I didn't like lying, but I wouldn't reveal my trip to the moors to speak to a powerful witch in case word got back to the royal family. "I was wondering about taking a short trip, but I was undecided. I like staying close to home. It's safer here."

"When you have to deal with a drunken fiancé with no manners and a heart of ice, you'll want to be on the opposite side of the world. Still, let's not talk about Jasper. I'll find some pleasantness while I'm here."

"It sounds as if you're not planning on staying for long."

"You never know how things will turn out. Deals break apart. Families who sell you realize their grave mistake and bargain to have you back. Drunken princes fall down stone staircases." Camilla giggled. "Wouldn't that be a hoot! A drunken Jasper ruins everything because he can't hold his drink. Still, look on the bright side. He'll be no use on the wedding night if he keeps drinking so much."

"I'd say a fall or a drunken misadventure on your special day would be terribly unfortunate. Prince Jasper needs to be careful."

"I should encourage him to drink more. At least when he's passed out drunk, he can't interfere with my fun." Camilla looked over her shoulder at the bustling market. "We should shop. I'll spend what's left of Jasper's money and then run away. Imagine the scandal."

I winced. "Um... forgive me for saying this, but it's forbidden to speak unkindly about any member of the royal family."

Camilla lightly slapped my arm. "You're so right, Bell. And so sensible. However, I have leeway into what I can get away with. The family thinks I'm their solution to their little... infertility issue. Would they be so foolish as to toss me into the dungeons for saying a few careless words?" She shook her head, her pale curls bobbing. "Careless words that are entirely true. I'll give them what they need when they show me the appropriate level of respect. Don't you agree?"

"I think you're brave," I said.

"What have I got to lose?"

"Your freedom? Maybe your life? The family holds public executions once a month."

"As if they'd dare to do something so scandalous to my perfect neck! My family would start a war against them. Well, I hope they would." Camilla pinched my arm. "Your concern for me is adorable but unnecessary. I hold the power."

I wasn't sure if Camilla was courageous or delusional. "I'm glad to hear it. If you'll excuse me, I really must go."

"No! Stay with me. Now, chastise me instantly."

I stared at her in alarm. "What for?"

"I said I wouldn't talk about my terrible love match, and here I am, twittering on about it as if I have nothing else to consider. Distract me. I insist upon it." Camilla grabbed my hand. "Where do people go in this village for entertainment?"

I slid a desperate glance at the portal entrance. If I didn't leave soon, my mission would have to be abandoned. "It depends on what you like to do. There's a wonderful bookstore."

"Reading is boring."

"How about places to eat?"

"I get everything I desire from the castle kitchen. Their cook is incredible."

"Alice is the best. We have parks and serene forest walks, providing you stick to the designated areas."

"I may have already mentioned I'm not a fan of exercise in any form."

"Museums?"

"No."

"Historic homes? There's a beautiful—"

"Tedious. I'm surrounded by history in that dreadfully cold stone tomb. Where do people go to dance?"

"The family holds private balls several times a year. I've never been to one, but I hear they're magnificent."

"Not that kind of dancing. They'll be stuffy affairs with formal dresses and stilted conversation. I went to plenty of balls when I first came out, and I almost expired from boredom." Camilla huffed out a breath. "I want to go somewhere where I can let my hair down and laugh."

"The village hall has a monthly dance. It's nothing special, though."

"Is there live music?"

"Always."

"And food and drink?"

"Of course. But—"

"When's the next one?"

"I believe it's at the end of the month."

"Then we shall go."

I failed to hide my surprise. "I can't! And there are more appropriate places for you to visit. The village dance gets rowdy. Prince Jasper could show you around and introduce you to more exclusive venues."

"That would hardly be fun." Camilla heaved out a sigh and looked away. "I have no friends here. I'm alone with a hateful man and a monstrous family. I detest it. I'm miserable."

"Things will improve," I said. "Once you're focused on your children, you'll barely notice Prince Jasper and the rest of the family."

"I hope that's true. But in the meantime, I must find something to entertain me. Please, help me. You're the only one who has shown me a trace of kindness since I arrived in this barren, dragonless place."

"You must have assistants who can support you."

"I have plenty of staff, but everyone tells me what I want to hear, rather than tell me the truth. And if I say a bad word about Jasper or anyone else in that horrible family, they look at me as if I'm insane. They must know what he's like. And I've been hearing terrible things about his brother. I'm glad he's not here. We would not be friends."

"Prince Godric is a special character," I said. "I'm sure he's enjoying his life at sea."

Camilla's laugh was hollow. "As if he went off and did anything so heroic. He probably got drunk and turned around in some terrible brothel. I hope he stays there, rotting from some incurable malady that has turned his manly parts black."

I didn't hide my smile quickly enough, and joined Camilla in a quiet laugh.

"The few times I met him, I came away feeling queasy. There's something about Godric that's unnatural." Camilla shook her head. "Although he hates Jasper, so we have that in common."

I looked around, but fortunately, no one was listening to this treasonous conversation, although there were curious eyes focused on us.

Camilla stopped walking and looked at her feet. "These shoes are so uncomfortable. I should commission a pair of those sensible flat boots you stomp around in. They're the ugliest shoes I've ever seen, but I'm sure they don't give you blisters."

"They are comfortable, even if they aren't the height of fashion," I said.

"That's what I'll do this afternoon. Is there a cobbler in the village?"

"Yes. Go past the bookstore, the bakery, and the apothecary, and Fanny Dewey will look after you. Oh, but perhaps you could ask someone at the castle? The family has tailors, and they only use companies that pay to display their royal seal of approval."

"No, a local cobbler is what I want. A sensible, practical woman who won't bow to me and tell me what she thinks I want to hear." Camilla playfully pinched my arm again. "Oh, I have a genius idea. I'll go in disguise like a common cleaner."

"I... why would you do that?"

She studied my clothing. "I can get some tatty old thing like you're wearing, and Fanny won't know who I am. It'll be fun. And imagine her surprise when she discovers she's making a pair of boots for a future princess."

"I'm glad it'll keep you entertained," I said. "Now, I really must go."

"I'll allow it, since you've helped me decide how I'll entertain myself this afternoon." Camilla leaned in close, her breath smelling of lemon drops. "However, doing things alone is unacceptable for a woman of my standing. On my next outing, you're coming with me."

I gently eased my elbow out of her grasp. "As wonderful as that sounds, I have very little time off."

She waved a hand in the air. "I'll fix it so you're free from your lowly shackles of dust and dirt. I'll tell Jasper I need a chaperone."

My composure almost slipped. "There are castle staff who would be happy to accompany you."

"No! I want you. And I shall have you as my chaperone. Worry not. I'll arrange everything." Camilla danced away before I could make any more excuses.

Hodgepodge appeared out of my pocket and clambered up my chest and onto my shoulder. "I'd rather face a mean, murderous moor witch than a crazy fiancée desperate for a friend. You spend too much time with Camilla, and she'll ruin you."

I nodded, dread spearing through me like a poisoned holly branch. "But how can we stop Camilla from demanding my company?"

Chapter 11

I only had to walk a short way before I reached the portal tunnel. At first sight, the rock appeared unremarkable, but as soon as I pressed my hand against it, an entrance opened.

It was the way into an elaborate portal tunnel system that let users get to almost anywhere in any magical realm, provided that the realm had an active portal tunnel. People traveled many thousands of miles in the blink of an eye using this incredible system.

If the Ithric family could, I had no doubt they'd shut it, but it was an essential part of the economic system, and to limit its use would mean their ruin.

My wrist gently pulsed as the magic activated, and I quietly whispered my destination.

Hodgepodge sat firmly on my shoulder as the magic activated, and I only had to take a few steps forward before low-growing shrubs, damp grasses, and springy bog moss surrounded me. The intense tang of wet, peaty soil filled my nose, and a thick, damp mist swirled around us. I checked to make sure I knew the location of the portal tunnel should we need to flee and then looked around.

This wasn't a moor cultivated by a person's hand but a wild, rich environment, full of twisty clumps of vibrant heather, giant pods of trees, and irregular shaped rocks that were testament to hundreds of years of growth interlaced with old magic. Magic maybe even the Ithric family feared.

"Astrid said, once we got here, we'd be able to feel magic," I whispered.

"I don't know about feel it, but I can hear something. It's coming up on us fast." Hodgepodge leapt nimbly from my shoulder and landed in a pile of dry heather. His head emerged, and he shook himself free.

"What do you hear?" I asked.

"Footsteps, and they're coming this way." Hodgepodge growled. "Stay back. It could be the witch."

A trickle of fear snaked down my spine. This part of the moorland was notorious as a hideout for bandits, criminals, and those wanted by the family for their illegal use of magic. There were no rules here, and although I'd worn the ring of strength Elara had gifted me, it would be no use against a powerful magic-wielding witch with an attitude.

"They're getting closer," Hodgepodge said. "Any second now and we should see them."

I could hear the footsteps, too. "There's more than one of them. Or maybe..."

A horse trotted into view, and Hodgepodge lunged.

I caught him mid-jump and cradled him against my chest as I stepped back from the horse. "Hey, boy. I hope we didn't startle you. What brings you out this way?"

The horse studied us for several seconds, his large dark eyes unblinking. He turned, flicked his tail, and trotted away.

"He's probably an enchanted horse. Or a hexed horse. Never trust a hexed horse," Hodgepodge said as he returned to his favorite spot on my shoulder.

"How do you know he's hexed?" I maintained a safe distance from the horse to avoid any back hoof action but followed him as he led us toward a glowing clump of thick-ferned trees. Trees that had no place in a moorland.

"That's the tricky bit," Hodgepodge said. "You never know which ones are hexed and which ones are just mean and want to kick you in the gut with a hoof."

"This one seems friendly. He's a helper horse."

"You won't think it's so helpful when he turns and bites you with those enormous teeth."

"Let's give him no reason to do that, shall we?"

We continued our path for ten minutes before entering the trees. The horse picked up speed, and I swiftly lost sight of him. Maybe he hadn't been helping, after all. "Which way now?"

"Back home," Hodgepodge said.

"We're here now."

"It's not too late to turn back."

My gaze settled on a pile of old clothing. As I walked closer to the heap, it turned out to be a living, breathing person. At least, I hoped they were living.

"Careful," Hodgepodge cautioned. "Nothing is what it seems on these moors. And the trees are vibrating. That's not normal."

I hurried closer. "Hello! Are you hurt? Was that your horse? Did he throw you?"

There was a groan from the pile of clothes, and a face appeared. It was a haggard old woman, with deep lines cut into her face and stringy grey hair hanging by her cheeks.

"Do you need help to get up? Or can I contact someone? A relative, perhaps." I heeded Hodgepodge's warning and made sure not to get too close to the old woman.

"Just a hand up, deary." The words scraped out of her dry throat. "I need a moment to get my bearings."

"Of course. What are you doing out here on your own?" I assisted the woman first to roll into a seated position and then got her on her feet. She was skin and bones, her clothes filthy and torn, with the smell of ripe cheese emanating from her body.

"There's nowhere else for me to go. The moor is my home." She glanced at Hodgepodge. "Who've you got there?"

"This is Hodgepodge, my companion. I'm Bell."

"A pleasure to meet you both. And I appreciate the help." Her eyes glowed purple as she continued her thorough visual inspection of both of us. "Most people would walk on by if they saw me in distress."

"They're wrong to do so," I said. "If that was your horse, I may be able to bring him back, and you can ride home."

"Double kindness. What a treat." The woman's intense gaze fixed on me. "What are you expecting in return?"

"Nothing! Well, you may be able to help me find someone who lives around here, but that's all."

"Do you seek someone who lives on the moor? Only the defeated, broken, or mind boggled live out here."

I nodded. "And we have little time to find them."

"Time is relative here. Use the portal to your advantage."

I was aware time shifts were common when traveling in the portals, but it was magic I rarely used and didn't know how to manipulate it.

"Do you know that the only folk who live around here are usually up to no good?" The woman snorted through her long, crooked nose. "Well, if you believe the lies our precious royal family peddle."

"I have heard this is a place for the disaffected," I said. "I'm hoping the woman we seek will assist us in solving a murder."

"Murder! Who died? Please say it was Lady Isolda. When her head is mounted upon a pole, it'll be a happy day. I'll dance around the moor and shoot fire balls into the sky."

"As far as I'm aware, Lady Isolda is very much alive. It's not a member of the family, but someone who used to work for them."

"Oh! I'm not interested in that." She turned and shuffled away.

"Wait! Before you leave, can you tell me where I can find Sabine Charming?"

"What do you want with her?" The woman kept shuffling through dry leaves.

"Do you know her?"

"She'll lead you to trouble. I suppose you've heard the rumors about her."

"I understand she's a powerful witch." I followed behind the woman, trekking deeper past the unnaturally tall trees that had no place on a moor.

"You want nothing to do with her. She's as mean as a stepped-on snake."

"I only need a few moments of her time. She knows the man who was killed."

The old woman paused from her shuffling. "What was this man's name?"

"Augustus Doubleday. He used to work for—"

The woman's form shimmered. There was a puff of smoke, and a strong smell of ashes filled the air. The old woman was gone, and a striking-looking woman in her fifties with a mane of red curls stood before us. "Has the idiot finally gone and gotten himself killed?"

"Sabine?" I asked.

"Don't look so surprised. Anyone who stumbles into my territory has to be tested."

"You were faking being a weak old crone?"

"Most simply ignore me. They think the stupid old woman on the ground has gotten herself in trouble or is already dead. Not you. You helped." That fiery gaze roved over me again. "And it seems you're doing it again with Augustus. You said he was murdered?"

"Yes, and I'd like to talk to you. I understand you and Augustus were close."

"Hah! By close, you mean he'd been seeing me for over a year without his simple-minded wife knowing. Then yes, we were close."

"What did you see in him?" Hodgepodge asked.

Sabine cackled a laugh. "It's not all about appearance. Augustus had charm about him. I wouldn't say he was the brightest man I'd ever encountered, but he was interesting. He liked to listen more than he talked. That's a rare quality in a man." She gestured for us to follow her and then turned and swept through the crunchy leaves. "Don't get me wrong, he had plenty of foibles. He drank too much. He had a growing paunch I was always telling him off about, and wandering eyes, which is how we came to know each other."

"I am sorry for your loss," I said.

"Don't be. He was much fonder of me than I was of him. He was someone to spend time with. A curiosity I kept and summoned now and again to amuse myself with."

"You're not sad he's dead?"

"I'm mildly aggrieved. We had a good thing going, and he was well paid for his work at the castle, so he always brought magnificent feasts whenever he came to stay. I liked that about him best. Augustus got the finest food." Sabine laughed to herself, one hand resting on her stomach. "He once bragged that he had better connections than the Ithric family, and I could well believe that. He had fingers in lots of pies. Still, no use having dead fingers in anything, is there? What happened to the silly old fool?"

"You may want to be sitting when I tell you."

"Nothing much startles me these days. Living out here, you get used to the weird and wonderful. I always imagined it would be the drink that got him." Sabine turned. "This way. My home is close. We can sit and talk about foolish men and the trouble they bring to themselves. Did he fall into a well and was too drunk to get out? No, I expect he gorged himself to death. That man could eat!"

"Nothing like that. How connected are you to what's going on at the castle?" I asked.

"I keep my ear to the ground, but I stay far away from that place. If Lady Isolda ever caught me poking around, I'd be done for. Well, she'd do her best to undo me, but she wouldn't get far." Sabine glanced over her shoulder. "Why? Is the revolution finally happening to oust that hostile family from a throne they never deserved to sit upon?"

"Stone statues have been showing up, and Lady Isolda is putting them in the chamber with the dragons."

"Of course she would. Spent a fortune on them, I suppose. Augustus complained the Ithric family spend like they own all the planet's magical resources, yet they have the income of a woodland mouse."

"I don't think she's paying for them. The statues are being made by magic."

"Oh! That puts a new slant on things. Go on." Sabine lifted her arms, and a small moss-covered hut appeared in front of us. "Come in. Home sweet home, if you don't mind regular invasions of moor toads and rude gremlins."

I had to duck to get through the entrance and entered the gloomy interior. Sabine snapped her fingers and numerous candles sprung to light, adding a welcoming glow to the hallway.

"At first, I thought it was someone making statues in the likeness of people around the court. Augustus's statue appeared a few days ago," I said.

"And?" Sabine shrugged off her cloak and hung it on a peg by the door before ushering us along the narrow hallway and into a tiny kitchen, the surfaces littered with pots and bottling jars. A strong smell of fermenting food lingered.

"I learned they weren't just statues. People had been turned into stone."

Sabine's eyes widened, a purple light blazing in them. "That's serious magic someone is messing with. Augustus died when he was trapped in the stone?"

"He died when someone pushed over his statue, and it shattered."

"Well, I never." She smacked a hand against her thigh. "What a way to go. He would never have seen that one coming."

"When was the last time you saw Augustus?" I settled into the chair Sabine pointed at, Hodgepodge sitting on my lap.

"It's been a while. Months. I forget exactly."

"You were no longer dating?"

"Only when it was at my convenience." Sabine collected a jug of dark green-colored liquid with twigs floating on the surface and poured us both a cup, pushing one over to me.

"You don't seem upset he's dead." I sniffed the liquid. It smelled of honey and something earthy I couldn't identify.

"You don't see me dancing around with joy, do you? This is me being sad."

"His statue was destroyed two nights ago. Do you remember what you were doing then?"

Sabine sniffed. "Checking for my alibi, are you?"

"I don't want to cause offense, but it would be good if we could discount you from the investigation."

"Investigation! Are you working for the royal guard?"

"No, but I found Augustus's statue destroyed. I'd like to know what happened to him."

"Got a good heart, I suppose."

"The best heart," Hodgepodge said. "There's no one better than Bell."

Sabine shrugged. "I spend most of my time alone. It's hard to make friends when everyone is a vagabond or a troublemaker who'll rob the mushrooms from your pantry if left alone."

"That must get lonely," I said.

"I manage fine." Sabine swirled her drink. "I was in the woods, foraging for toxic mushrooms. They're highly prized, though forbidden by the family. Although I've sold my special mushroom blend to a royal family member a time or two." She chuckled to herself.

"You forage at night?" I asked. "Doesn't that make it harder to find the mushrooms?"

"They conceal themselves in the daylight. Sunlight shrivels the skin." Sabine arched an eyebrow as she scrutinized my face. "You don't believe me? Here, I'll show you what I collected." She went to a small cupboard and lifted out an earthenware pot, set it on the table, and eased off the lid. "Be careful not to breathe too deeply. The fumes make many lightheaded."

I peeked inside and discovered an array of mushrooms. Although it proved Sabine had collected mushrooms within the last few days, I couldn't tell when the collection had taken place, so her alibi was of little use to me.

"Did you and Augustus have any disagreements recently?" I gently pushed away the earthenware pot full of mushrooms. The fumes reminded me of sour grapes and dragon gas, and my eyes watered.

"Now and again." Sabine settled back in her seat. "Don't point the finger of blame at me, though. If I'd wanted Augustus dead, I could have invented a dozen ways to destroy him. I wouldn't have gone to the trouble of turning him into stone and smashing his statue. I'd want to see the fear in his eyes when I did it."

"Turned him into a toad and squashed him under your boot?" Hodgepodge asked.

Sabine cackled a laugh. "Wouldn't that be entertaining? But, no. There are bogs and shady holes in these moors that I take people to when I want them to disappear. Make sure you stay on my good side, or you'll find yourself there with no way out."

Hodgepodge leapt onto the table and hissed at her. "Don't threaten Bell!"

Sabine hooked him up in one hand, and a shimmer of brilliant magic surrounded him. I cried out in alarm as Hodgepodge doubled in size, then doubled again, growing ever larger until he burst through the roof, transforming into his giant wyvern form.

I staggered back to avoid being squashed by his feet, and he stared at me with big eyes, both of us stunned by his transformation.

Sabine laughed again as she stared up at him. "I knew there was something different about you two. What a beautiful creature. So unique. Not a dragon. Something else. No matter, he's wonderful. How much do you want for him?"

I caught hold of one of Hodgepodge's giant front limbs and stepped onto his foot, so he wouldn't tread on me. "He's not for sale. Hodgepodge is my best friend."

Sabine scowled at me. "If you let me have him, I'll tell you a secret about the Ithric family. Something they don't want anyone to know about. How about it? Let's make a deal. Your creature for my secret."

Chapter 12

I gripped Hodgepodge's leg, glad to be protected from the falling roof tiles and crumbling wood that rained down around us. "I wouldn't trade Hodgepodge for anything."

"What about gold? Any amount. I know someone who makes it. Spins it out of twine," Sabine said.

"No! You could offer me my own castle, a dungeon full of gold, and a tame unicorn, and I'd still refuse you. Hodgepodge is priceless to me. He's stood by me through dark times, trials, and the risk of death. I've never had such a loyal friend."

"I will find something to turn your head." Sabine strode around Hodgepodge, taking in every glorious scaled inch of him. "Perhaps you seek true love. I could summon your soulmate. A strapping farmer, perhaps? No, you strike me as a woman who'd like a man who could keep up with your sensibilities and curiosity. Although, I'd be sure to make him handsome. How does that sound?"

Hodgepodge tried to poke his head through the hole in the roof but smashed his chin on broken tiles. He grumbled and huffed, smoke blooming from his nostrils. "I'm stuck!"

"Hang in there. I'm figuring things out," I yelled up at him.

"If you give him to me, I'll return him to his normal size," Sabine said. "Although he is truly wonderful in his giant form. Can he breathe fire?"

"It's no business of yours what he can do," I said. "We belong to each other. We found each other during a dark moment and formed an unbreakable bond. No amount of gold or handsome men will change that."

"A loan, then. I'll have Hodgepodge on the weekends. I could ride him for miles and have no fear that anyone from the royal family would bother me. They'd be too busy staring open-mouthed at the magnificent beast I controlled."

"Nobody controls me, you wee radge." Hodgepodge's voice was a deep rumble in his chest. "I'm my own creature."

"And you will be your own creature with me, you fine fellow," Sabine said. "Talk sense to your companion. My secret is not something I share easily, but it'll give you a new light on the twisted family who have their claws sunk into this once delightful realm. Wouldn't you like to know it? Maybe it can help you solve the puzzle about Augustus's death."

"Why would it do that?" I asked.

Amusement danced in Sabine's eyes. "I see I've tempted you."

I gritted my teeth. I wanted to know what happened to Augustus and if it was connected to the stone heart amulet but not at the expense of losing Hodgepodge. "We'll find another way to solve this mystery."

"I'll give you a moment to reconsider," Sabine said.

"Then what?" Hodgepodge stamped a foot, making the floor shake. "You'll imprison us in some twisted magical prison?"

"I could if I wanted to. No one would ever find you out here." Sabine wriggled her fingers, magic sparking on her palm. "I've yet to decide whether you were brave or foolish to take this trip. Obviously, I sensed the power in you, Hodgepodge, but Bell is a mystery. There's something about you that is different, too, and I see the magic ring glimmering on your finger, but it's more than that."

"I know how to use this ring," I said. "I don't want to hurt you, but if you trap us here, you'll leave me no choice."

"And I'll stomp you," Hodgepodge said.

"Calm yourself, scaled one," Sabine said. "If I had a mind to, I could destroy both of you in the blink of an eye."

"We came here for answers, not trouble." I flexed my fingers. I didn't want to do battle with this witch. She exuded a primal power that I'd never encountered before, even when magic was freely used within the realm. I wouldn't stand a chance against her, but if she tried to take Hodgepodge, I'd fight back. I'd fight until the very last breath left my body.

Sabine raised her hands, her palms covered in a liquid sprawl of magic. She thrust up, and the magic covered Hodgepodge. He roared then returned to normal size.

I ran toward him and gathered him into my arms.

"Run! Sabine is super powerful. We need to leave now," he hissed out.

I turned to the door. Sabine blocked it, but she made no move to attack.

"Let us pass."

"Be still and patient. I don't really want your Hodgepodge. Although he is an incredible creature," she said.

"If you don't want him, open the door and allow us to leave," I said. "I made a mistake by coming here."

"Soon. And relax. I was testing you." Sabine stepped away from the door. "I needed to know if you were truly loyal to each other. So many people say what they think you want to hear, rather than revealing the truth, no matter how painful. They cower before the Ithric family, and lies slip from their mouths like poisoned honey. Their actions reveal their beliefs, though."

"I don't lie," I said.

"Neither do I, you crabbit witch." Hodgepodge blasted a string of Scottish cuss words into the air.

Sabine inclined her head. "I apologize for over-stepping. The energy pulsing from you intrigued me, and I wanted to see what you were. And what a delight." She walked away from the door, settled back in her seat, and sipped the green liquid. "Both of your hearts are pure, even if there is dragon stink about you."

I'd been making for the door, determined to leave, but those words made me pause. "You don't like dragons?"

"What's to like? They left us. When we needed their support the most, they weren't around."

I placed my hand on the door. "Perhaps they had no choice but to leave."

"What makes you say that? Since you smell like one, you must be around them. But there are none here."

"What if there were?" I asked.

"Then I would have words. Tell them it's intolerable to leave us in the wretched hands of the Ithric family. This realm is falling apart thanks to their malevolence."

"I don't disagree," I said.

"Bell, let's get out of here while we still can," Hodgepodge urged. "She could try to trick us again."

"I'm done with my tricks, little one. But I am intrigued about your dragon knowledge." Sabine's eyes glowed an intense purple. "If you tell me everything about them, I'll share my secret with you."

I took a step toward her. "No more surprises?"

"I can't promise that, but if there is, they will be good surprises. Do you like lemon cake?"

"Don't eat or drink anything she offers," Hodgepodge said.

"I'm not fae. I don't enchant my food and send people dancing in the stars until their feet bleed. Besides, I'm a terrible baker. I trade baked goods with a local nymph who lives a few miles from here. What she can do in the kitchen is nothing short of miraculous. She gets some of my foraged food, and I receive her cakes. They're delicious. Her lemon cake won awards."

Hodgepodge's stomach growled close to my ear, causing Sabine to laugh.

"No cake," I said. "But I will share information about the dragons."

"Then sit and talk." Sabine lifted her hand, and the scattering of wood and broken tiles rose from the floor.

Within a few minutes, the roof was repaired, and it was impossible to tell Hodgepodge had smashed through it.

"This one is too powerful for her own good," Hodgepodge whispered in my ear.

"I may be old, but my hearing is excellent," Sabine said. "And my power is the reason I was exiled."

I perched on the edge of the seat. "From what I understand, the Ithric family put large bounties on magic users' heads when they didn't obey the laws. Is that what happened to you?"

"They tried. Every bounty hunter failed to capture me, and I'd send them away with a warning in their ear not to come back. There were always a few new faces who didn't understand, but word soon spread that I was impossible to capture." Sabine's expression was one of smug satisfaction as she stood and walked to the kitchen counter, cut herself a large slice of lemon cake, and took a bite. "Are you sure I can't tempt you?"

Hodgepodge's stomach grumbled again, so I patted his side. "We're fine, thank you. Since the family couldn't capture you, they sent you here instead?"

"I decided I didn't enjoy living in a place where I was always looking over my shoulder," Sabine said. "It got tiring having to fight every day. I chose to come here."

"That's your secret?" Hodgepodge asked.

"Oh, no, little one." The glow in her eyes intensified. "My secret is that the Ithric family pays me to stay away. And they pay generously. I'm not the only one. There must be thirty of us living on the moors who receive a stipend every month to cause no trouble and not reveal their powerful front is false."

I stared at her with wide eyes. "They've declared themselves the most powerful magical ruling family in existence. No one can beat their magic. And they have a collection room full of magical artifacts and books full of spells that make them virtually indestructible."

"If that's so, why has Lady Isolda and her crazy husband decreed only a limited few should have access to magic? If they're so strong, they wouldn't fear other people using magic. No, it's a front." Sabine tipped her chair back. "The average magic user may believe the lies and propaganda they spout. The rest of us, they pay for our silence. Trust me, I'm not the only one they fear."

"They collected magic items to ensure no one else can use them against them?" I asked.

"I imagine so. Take away the enchanted objects, and it means no one else can have them. That's my secret. Now tell me yours," Sabine said. "I need to know why you smell of both bleach and dragon smoke."

I drew in a breath and let it out slowly. I'd rather have Sabine on my side than an enemy. If I could convince her the dragons were still noble, but they needed help, she may offer assistance.

"I grow older sitting here. Tell me your story and be quick about it," Sabine said.

"I'm a cleaner in the castle. I work in the stone chamber with the dragon statues."

"That explains the bleach. What about the dragon stink?"

I gripped Hodgepodge, and he wrapped his tail around my wrist in a show of support. "Emberthorn and Stormwing are alive."

Sabine dismissed my words with a hand. "Don't tease me, deary. They died. There was public mourning for weeks after their tragic loss."

"Their deaths weren't accidental," Hodgepodge said. "The family found a weakness, a way to defeat them. They no longer wanted to rule with the dragons. They weakened Emberthorn and Stormwing and then destroyed them. But they made a big mistake."

I nodded. "They kept their bones. Just like they've hoarded all powerful magical objects, they knew there was immense power in the bones, but they didn't know how to harness it. They stored the bones inside the statues. When the statues activated—"

Sabine held out a hand, the palm facing me. "Activated how?"

"With a blood sacrifice," I said. "To be precise, my blood. Some of my blood got smeared on Emberthorn, and it woke him. I've been working with someone at the castle to restore their strength so they can flee. Sabine, the dragons were never dead, only slumbering. I'm bringing them back."

Sabine was still as stone as she absorbed the information, and then laughter boomed out of her. "Sweet revenge. The family's tyranny is over at last."

"Um... There's a long way to go before that happens, but I'm hopeful things are changing for the better."

"Yes, things will change once the dragons are back. The family will run in terror. For all their benevolence, dragons can be vengeful creatures. Stormwing is especially so. This is wonderful news."

"Yet marred by the problem of the stone statues appearing," I said. "We believe someone has acquired the stone heart amulet. Does that mean anything to you?"

Sabine's smile dropped like a tossed rock into a bottomless cavern. "You know this for a fact?"

"I haven't seen the amulet, but when Augustus was destroyed, there was an enchanted rune stone among the remains. Friends of mine identified it as a marker for the amulet. Statues are being created every day, encasing people who work at the castle. It has to be someone with extremely powerful magic who can create so many statues."

Sabine gulped and set down the last of the cake she'd been about to eat. "Whoever has that amulet could even defeat me. I would like it myself to wreak revenge. This is terrible news."

"It was one of the objects held by the family," I said. "I'm concerned it could be someone already in a position of power using it."

"A family member? This is bad. This is very bad." Sabine stood and paced the small kitchen. "You need to stay away from this. If you get hit by the amulet, you could spend eternity as a stone statue. That's assuming someone doesn't smash you to pieces like Augustus. That magic is dark and wrong. I rarely agree that magical objects should be contained, but I've always supported its destruction."

"I'm with you there," I said. "If a member of the Ithric family has it, I'm not sure how I'll be able to stop them."

"Same here, deary," Sabine said. "You have a dangerous snake slithering around that castle. Make sure it doesn't bite you."

Chapter 13

Sabine had fretted about the stone heart amulet for several minutes, and although I'd directed her back to Augustus's murder, she wasn't moving from the topic.

I checked the time and gasped. "I need to leave! I'll be late for work."

"Of course, of course." Sabine grabbed my hand and squeezed it. "Bell, it took great courage to question me. I had no problem with Augustus. He was a foolish, arrogant man, and I can't say I grieve his loss, but I wish you well on your quest. It won't be easy to bring down whoever is using the stone heart amulet."

I nodded my thanks. "I really must go. If a family member notices I'm missing—"

"Allow me. I can get you back to the castle faster than the portal tunnels."

Before I could question what Sabine intended to do, a hot gust of wind blasted around us, and what felt like icy raindrops pounded against my skin for several seconds. When the wind died down, I found myself with Hodgepodge back at the castle.

Hodgepodge shuddered and shook himself from head to tail. "That is one witch I don't want to meet again."

I shook out my skirts and patted myself over to check everything was where it should be. "Sabine has incredible power. It's no wonder the family pays her to stay away. I'm certain, if she set her mind to it, she could destroy them by clicking her fingers." I took a moment to get my bearings then dashed around the side of the castle and into the servants' entrance.

"Can we trust her, though?" Hodgepodge asked. "Power of that magnitude often leads to an unstable character. And I still haven't forgiven her for grabbing me."

"That was rude." I dashed along the chilly tunnel. "Sabine has no alibi to speak of. She showed us those mushrooms, but she could have picked them any time. It sounds like she's a loner, keeps to herself as much as possible, which means it's unlikely anyone saw her foraging."

"Even if they did, we're not going back to find out if she was snooping around the woodland looking for dangerous mushrooms or sneaking into the castle to kill her former lover. If we returned to the moor, we'd only end up in a more dangerous situation. Probably stumble across a deranged moor nymph who'd force-feed us her poisoned cake."

"That lemon cake did look amazing."

Hodgepodge grumbled to himself. "Ach, that it did. Better miss out on cake than die from mushroom poisoning."

I hurried into the main hallway and collected my cleaning equipment. "We need to find out if Sabine was telling the truth about the last time she saw Augustus. She acted as if their relationship was a passing fancy and they hadn't been seeing each other regularly, but I'm not sure if that was true."

Hodgepodge clung to my shoulder as I dashed along. "She was scared of the stone heart amulet."

"So am I. The amulet is ancient. It must have been used thousands of times, and it grew stronger with every use. It's no wonder Sabine was concerned about encountering it." I paused by the door, relieved to see a few visitors still in the chamber who were lingering for a few more minutes before the session ended. We'd made it back in the nick of time.

"We can't dismiss Sabine as a suspect," Hodgepodge said.

"If she is innocent, she could be a valuable ally," I said.

"Or our worst enemy."

The last of the visitors left the chamber, and I hurried in. I'd barely set down my cleaning equipment before the main door opened. Camilla dashed in, a gleeful expression on her face. Hodgepodge slithered away and hid behind my mop bucket.

"There you are! I have a surprise for you."

"What's that?" I asked.

"After our encounter in the market, I went straight to Jasper and demanded you have the rest of the day off." She clapped her hands together. "Guess what? He said yes. I have so many plans. We're going to eat, shop, try on pretty dresses, and more. And we must do something with that dreadful hair."

"That's kind of you, but I have duties here." I gestured to the offerings visitors had left behind.

"No! You must come with me. I have everything arranged."

"It's so generous of you to offer. But I must decline."

Camilla's brilliant blue eyes hardened. "You cannot decline me. I'm almost your princess. Don't you want to spend the afternoon with me? If you're worried about money, you don't need to be. I have plenty. Well, Jasper will give me some."

"It's not that, although I rarely have the funds to buy anything pretty."

"I see that! I've seen you in the same dress several days in a row. I'm amazed you don't smell like a mangy dog." Camilla wrinkled her nose. "There is a whiff of mildew in the air. Or is it gas? Such an odd scent. It matters not. We will burn that thing you're wearing."

I ducked my head. It was my favorite dress. "I do my best with the little I have."

"Don't be offended. Think of this as a kindness. I'll relieve you of your shabby attire and buy you something nice. Something you won't be ashamed to be seen in."

"And again, your generosity knows no bounds, but—"

Camilla screamed. Not a small scream of frustration, but an all-out high-pitched bellow that had me clapping my hands over my ears as the piercing shriek echoed around the chamber.

A few seconds later, the main door was heaved open, and armed guards raced in. There were four of them, and they all held sparking sticks in their hands. Warwick was among them.

"My lady, is there a problem?" Warwick's gaze cut to me, even though he addressed Camilla, and his eyes narrowed.

"She won't do as I tell her," Camilla said. "I have offered Bell an afternoon of delights, and she said no.

She would rather clean this place than have anything to do with me."

"That's not what I meant," I said. "If I don't look after the chamber, no one else will."

"What's going on?" Prince Jasper appeared in the doorway, a frown on his face. "Camilla, was that you who screamed?"

"Because no one is listening to me as usual," Camilla said. "I want Bell to chaperone me this afternoon. I told you that was what I wanted. You said yes. Don't you remember?"

"Of course. I can't imagine why you want a cleaner as your chaperone, but I've already said you can borrow her." Prince Jasper strode in, his expression thunderous.

I curtsied in front of him. "I have a responsibility to the stone chamber."

"No, no, you don't. At least, not for today. My sweet fiancée requested your company. It's all been arranged, and the chamber will be looked after in your absence. You're not such a valuable asset that we can't find someone else to clear the detritus the peasants leave behind." Prince Jasper kicked over a candle, spilling hot wax across the stone.

"You see! You have nothing to worry about. You won't lose your boring little job. Oh! Was that your concern? I don't expect there's much work to be had around here. Cleaning has no skill, after all. You have my word that the dirt will be here for you tomorrow." Camilla grabbed my hand. "I didn't mean to be angry with you, but I was so looking forward to my afternoon away from the castle doing fun things. Having girl time. No men allowed, if you understand."

"An appropriate chaperone will accompany you," Prince Jasper said.

"You're not coming with us," Camilla said.

"I'm not. That would not be appropriate. I'm a prince, not a watch guard." His tight expression showed exactly how unhappy he was to be talked down to by Camilla. "You will have an escort. Warwick has selected some of his best men."

"I don't want anxious guards listening in and spoiling our fun," Camilla said.

"My lady, my guards are professional. We will remain at a discreet distance, and you will barely see us. But it is unwise for you to walk around the village without protection," Warwick said.

She heaved out a sigh and rolled her eyes. "Very well. Jasper, give Bell money. I don't want her feeling like she's too poor to be seen with me."

Prince Jasper took out a pouch from inside his tailored tunic and tossed it at me. "Enjoy yourself. Make sure my fiancée is thoroughly entertained."

I had no other excuses to make. If I continued to defy Camilla, she'd become more upset, and I'd risk being shoved in the dungeon for disobedience.

I smiled. "I'm very much looking forward to this sudden change of plans."

Camilla squeaked and bounced on her toes. "We'll have so much fun and become lifelong friends, I just know it."

I reached for my cleaning equipment, hoping to see where Hodgepodge had concealed himself, but Camilla yanked me away. "Forget that. I'll have someone take care of your things. Jasper, deal with Bell's belongings. She appears very attached to her mop and buckets."

"Of course, my love." He clicked his fingers, and a guard sprang into action.

"Please put the things in the cleaning closet in the main hallway. Do you know where that is?" I asked him.

"I'll ensure everything is as it should be," Warwick muttered. "If you know what's good for you, you'll stop dawdling and not leave Camilla waiting any longer." His face showed no expression other than the brief arch of an eyebrow. It was all the warning I needed as I allowed myself to be hauled out of the stone chamber by an excitable Camilla.

Hodgepodge had cleverly hidden himself somewhere, but I had no concerns about him abandoning me. He'd be close, keeping watch, and making sure I stayed safe.

"This will be the best day ever," Camilla announced as we stepped outside the castle, Warwick and three other guards close behind. "Let's start at the dress shop. I must get you out of those shabby things and into something formfitting. With all that physical labor, I imagine you have a nice figure hiding under the drab."

"I really couldn't say," I said.

"You must. You really must say whatever you want." Camilla still had a tight grip on my hand, as if she feared I'd change my mind and run back to the chamber. It was an appealing idea. "I'm so tired of having to watch what I say in front of Lady Isolda. Isn't she terrifying? Beautiful, but her moods are unpredictable. It seems her husband isn't the only one with a few bats in the belfry knocking things loose."

"She has royal bearing. That can feel intimidating." Everyone was watching as Camilla marched us through the marketplace, heading towards Tilly's dress shop.

"That's your polite way of saying she terrifies the underdrawers off you, too. She's to be my mother-in-law! Heavens forbid. I don't suppose it's too late to call the whole thing off, is it?" Her laugh had an edge of hysteria about it, and there was a hint of desperation in her eyes. "No! Let's forget that horrible topic. I think you'd look ravishing in red. With that dark hair and pale skin, you'll look like Snow White. This way." Camilla pulled me into the dress shop.

I glanced over my shoulder. Warwick was smirking, but I was more interested in Hodgepodge, who was scuttling along the gutters of the shops on the opposite side of the street, keeping pace with us.

Camilla poked around the shop for several minutes, ably assisted by Tilly Wallace, who was happy to accept a pile of dresses into her outstretched arms, despite looking terrified at dealing with such an influential customer.

"This way," Camilla said. "I want you to try on all of these."

"They're for me?" I followed behind her, shooting an apologetic look at Tilly.

"Of course. I never buy anything ready-made. My gowns are custom fit. Hurry! I want a fashion show, and I want it now."

The next half an hour was a blur of being pulled in and out of dresses I could never afford in a million years. There were sleeveless ones, full-skirted ones, backless dresses, frilly dresses, so many colors and fabrics that I had a headache by the sixth change.

"I'll have the red one and the dark blue one," Camilla said while I was still getting dressed.

I shook my head as I tugged on my boots. "That's too much."

"I must buy you something."

"Really, there's no need."

"Don't make me scream again."

My head whipped up. "A pair of gloves will be fine."

"Gloves! She's so humble that it makes me sick," Camilla said to Tilly. "Both dresses, and I'll pay for them now. And I want to come in for a fitting. I'll need a dozen gowns. I'll have my measurements and style preferences sent to you."

"A dozen dresses! Of course. Whatever you desire." Tilly was beaming with delight as she rang up the order.

"Wear that one." Camilla pointed at the red dress as I stood from my seat.

"I'll keep it for a special occasion," I said.

"If you want to be seen with me, you must dress respectably," Camilla said. "Put it on. We're not leaving the shop until you do."

I dragged myself back into the changing room and rested my head against the wall. What had I gotten myself into?

"I'm hungry. We're going to eat next," Camilla called out. "Don't lace yourself in too tight. I plan to feast."

I struggled into the dress, bagged my old clothes, and walked out. The sleeves were lace and linked over my fingers. The neckline was plunging and left far too much skin exposed. At least I had my comfortable boots on, hidden under the swathes of ruched fabric.

Camilla selected a silky red shawl and draped it around me. "Perfect. Now, if I could just do something with your hair, I'd be able to take you everywhere. You're my perfect little doll. Tilly, do you sell cosmetics?"

"Just clothing."

"Do you have any of your own?"

"Of course."

"I'm using it on Bell."

I gulped. "I don't usually wear makeup."

"You do now." Camilla snapped her fingers. "Hurry. I'm a terrible grouch when I need to eat."

Tilly dashed over with a pouch of makeup. She held it out to Camilla.

Camilla shook her head. "You! You make her look nice. Less gutter grunge and more genteel courtesan."

"Oh. Of course." Tilly crouched in front of me.

"Just a little," I whispered to her. "Don't make me look painted."

She bit her lip as she covered me in color and puffed powder on my cheeks.

"Yes! So much better. I can barely recognize Bell." Camilla giggled. "She's almost as lovely as me. Let's go eat."

I trudged out of the shop, checking where Hodgepodge was. He clung to a nearby lamppost, his tail curled tight against his body.

"You look nice," Warwick muttered as he passed me.

I glared at him. "I feel ridiculous."

"We're going to the bakery." Camilla hurried ahead of us, and we had to dash to keep up with her speedy pace. By the time I got inside, she was placing an order at the counter, which the astonished-looking assistant was hurrying to fill.

Camilla turned to me. "I'm getting one of everything. We can share and swap cakes. Isn't that what best friends do?"

"I imagine so. That's a lot of cake, though."

She giggled again. "Jasper will have a fit if he finds out what I'm eating. He keeps warning me not to get fat, but I couldn't care less. Besides, isn't that what he wants me to do? Get fat with his child?"

The assistant behind the bakery counter made a startled noise in the back of his throat but kept piling the cakes into boxes.

"Well?" Camilla adjusted my shawl. "Should I care what my fiancé thinks of my figure? Isn't a happy relationship all about what a person makes you feel like on the inside?"

"It's been a while since I dated," I said, "but that makes sense."

"Doesn't it! And that's what I keep telling Jasper, but he doesn't listen. I should never have agreed to marry a man who had a silver spoon in his mouth when he arrived in this world."

I pressed my lips together, refusing to badmouth the family. Although Camilla was free with her words and her dislike of Prince Jasper, I still didn't trust her.

"Call one of the guards in to help." Camilla piled boxes of cake into my arms, and I headed to the door and handed them to a waiting guard. I returned and collected another two boxes. "Where would you like to eat?"

"I'd like to be outside. I want everyone to see me gorging and caring nothing about what the family thinks of me. You must gorge, too."

Camilla must have a death wish, but there was no way I could argue with her. "There's a public park close by. It's where the stone statues are kept before they're taken to the chamber. It could be interesting to see if there are any new additions."

"Still thinking about boring work, are we?" Camilla shook her head. "I suppose you're the one responsible for dusting them, so it's only reasonable."

"I am. And I really don't mind."

"You should. In that pretty dress I paid for, you'd almost pass as respectable. If we set our minds to it, we could find a suitable man for you to marry and give you a life of comfort. Certainly better than what you're currently enduring. Wouldn't you like that?"

"I endure my current situation very well. Let me show you to the park."

Camilla twittered on and made comments about the Ithric family, but I let it wash over me. I was glad to get to the park and picked a bench tucked in one corner. It would mean less public scrutiny.

Camilla didn't notice my deliberate choice of seating. She dumped down the single box she'd been carrying and flopped into the seat, flipping open the lid and scooping out a flaky pastry tart smothered in whipped cream. "What an afternoon, and we're just getting started. Now, if we're going to be best friends, you must be truthful with me. No more concealing things and making up lies."

"I'm not lying about anything," I said.

"I forbid you to hold your tongue any longer," Camilla said. "To show you I'm being truthful, I'll go first. I wish... I wish Jasper was dead!"

Chapter 14

I stared at Camilla. She stared back. Although there was a smile on her face, her gaze was serious. I opened my mouth, but no words came out.

"How should we do it?" She waved a hand in the air as a drowsy fly buzzed close. "Ugh! I've changed my mind. I hate being outside. I saw a rustic tavern nearby, and I doubt anyone from the castle will be in there, so we can talk about methods of murder with no snooping guards. And the walk will give you time to come up with ideas. I need at least five ways to dispose of him."

I had no time to protest as Camilla stood and strode away. I gathered the discarded boxes of cake, spotting a group of children nearby. I hurried over, leaving them delighted with the treats, then dashed after Camilla. Most of the guards were flanking her, but Warwick had fallen back.

"Be careful," he muttered. "Camilla's fragile, and being forced into this marriage could have tipped her over the edge."

"I've figured that out. She wants me to help her plan Prince Jasper's assassination."

Warwick narrowed his eyes. "It's not the worst idea I've ever heard."

"This isn't a joke. People have been killed for talking about less."

"If she insists on discussing it, keep your voice down. The family has people everywhere. Even in rustic little places you don't think they know about."

"I'm being discreet! But I can't say the same for Camilla. She'll get herself in serious trouble. She thinks her privileged status protects her, but it'll only get her so far before she's dragged into the dungeons and never seen again."

"Get control of her, Bell."

"How? I cautioned her, but she won't listen to reason."

"Then get her so drunk she can't string a sentence together."

"Bell! Stop flirting with the handsome guard and join me." Camilla had stopped walking and stood by the tavern entrance with her hands on her hips.

I hurried away from Warwick, gaining comfort from seeing Hodgepodge perched on the top of the tavern sign. He was always watching over me, even when he couldn't be wrapped around my neck.

Camilla clapped her hands together. "I'm so excited. I love these quaint little places and their backward ways. What shall we drink? I'll buy drinks for everyone, shall I?"

"We should keep this discreet. I'm not sure Lady Isolda would approve of you coming here."

Camilla snorted daintily, a tiny noise like a pixie sneezing. "She has no say over what I do. I'm marrying her dreadful son, not her."

I lifted one shoulder. "It's sort of the same thing. You marry one member of the Ithric family, and you're connected to all of them."

Camilla stamped her foot. "It's so frustrating. Very well, no drinks for all. The guards must stay out here, though. I don't want everyone staring at us and thinking we're an oddity for having weaponized chaperones."

"I'm sorry, but that won't be possible," Warwick said. "We're here for your safety. We can't guarantee that if we remain outside."

Camilla's sigh had a touch of the dramatics, and for a second, I thought she'd stamp her foot again. "Just you, since Bell is sweet on you. The rest remain outside."

Warwick briefly consulted with the other guards then nodded. He opened the door to the tavern and gestured us in.

Camilla bobbed into a small curtsy and giggled as she caught hold of my arm. "He's such a gentleman. I can see why you like him."

I shot a desperate look at Warwick, but there was nothing he could do to save me from this experience.

The walls of the tavern were painted a blood red. The floors and ceilings were black, and a small bar sat to the right of the entrance. There were a few afternoon drinkers in there, but other than that, the place was quiet. I was grateful. The fewer people who saw us in here, the better.

Camilla was looking around, her eyes bright with excitement. "I'm having cider. What do you want?"

"Nothing alcoholic this early in the day," I said.

"I'll get you a mead. They can put lemonade in it so it isn't strong." She looked around again. "Where's the server to take our drinks order and show us to our seats?"

"It's not that kind of place. We pick our own seats and go to the bar to order." I spotted a familiar face serving behind the bar and relaxed. Dolores Nickel, one of the women I'd rescued off the ship, raised her chin in acknowledgment, her expression full of curiosity as she realized who I was with.

"I'll pick our seats. You get the drinks." Camilla walked away, greeting everyone she passed with a small royal wave, her left hand creating circles in the air.

I hurried over to Dolores, acknowledging her raised eyebrows with a shrug and a what-can-I-do hand gesture.

"Well, look at you. You've gone up in the world," Dolores said.

"I'm hoping I'm in the middle of a nightmare," I said. "I'm not sure how it's happened, but Camilla wants us to be friends."

"On first-name terms with the royal princess bride." Dolores chuckled. "I knew there was something special about you when we met on that ship."

"The less said about that, the better," I whispered.

"Don't worry about me spreading gossip. What will it be?"

I ordered a cider and lemonade with a sprig of thyme in it for me. Dolores waved away the offer of money, even though I told her it was from Prince Jasper's coffers.

I was pleased to see Camilla had picked a discreet booth at the back of the tavern. She was seated so she could watch people come in and out, her back to the wall. Warwick stood a short distance away. I set our drinks down, and she instantly took a gulp of cider and had a coughing fit.

"Goodness! This is different." She drank some more. "Sharp apples. Lovely."

I sipped my drink. "You must be tired after everything we've done this afternoon."

"I live to shop! And eat. Once I've explored all the shops in this village, I plan to make trips elsewhere. You'll have to come with me."

"That sounds exciting." There was no point in arguing with Camilla, and I didn't want to be screamed at again.

"What have you come up with?" she asked.

"You've lost me." I was very much not lost, but I didn't want to have this conversation.

"What are we going to do about Jasper?" She tapped the back of my hand with a painted nail. "He lies and sneaks about. I don't trust him. And his mother is controlling. She's a dreadful woman. I'm certain she doesn't like me, but she has no choice but to keep me here. She's desperate for a royal child. Don't you think it's so tedious and old-fashioned? Why can't she pass the seat onto someone deserving, rather than simply because of the type of blood running through their veins?"

"Traditions are hard to break," I said.

"I'd break them if I was in control." Camilla gulped more cider. "I could get Jasper drunk and push him down the stairs or off one of the turrets. He's not muscular. He's too lazy to look after himself properly, so I should be able to push him off balance."

I failed to hide my alarm. "That sounds dangerous. What if you pushed him, and he grabbed you? You'd both fall to your deaths."

"Oh! I hadn't thought about that. How infuriating. I don't want to die. Poison?"

I shook my head. "You said Prince Jasper sneaks about. Where does he go?"

"I don't know. I'm just glad whenever he's not in the same room as me." Camilla's eyes widened. "We should follow him! What fun that would be. He's probably going to some awful knocking shop to satisfy his lust. It would be the kind of despicable thing he would do. He's always pawing at me and making demands, which I refuse to fulfill. Not until I have a ring on my finger will I go anywhere near his ghastly bedroom and submit to his gross, damp hands and moist lips. Have you noticed how moist his lips are?"

I sidestepped the question. "That sounds sensible."

"So, shall we follow him?"

I was figuring out how to avoid this suicide mission when the tavern door opened. A frigid hush fell over the customers. Lady Isolda stood in the doorway, a guard in her shadow. She strode toward us, her velvet cloak flapping behind her, and stopped by the table. "Camilla, I was surprised to learn you were here. It's not a place the family frequents."

Camilla stared back at her defiantly. "I'm exploring my new home. There's no law against that, is there?"

"Of course not, my dear. But you should be resting. And you missed an appointment with our healer. Leah was concerned something had happened to you when you didn't arrive. We need to ensure you remain healthy."

Camilla's bottom lip jutted out. "I despise being force-fed her potions. They do me no good. I'm as fertile as a pure-bred unicorn. When the time is right, I'll give you what you need."

"Of that, I have no doubt." Lady Isolda's gaze skated to me as she took away the glass of cider. "You have a new friend?"

I hadn't taken a breath since Lady Isolda appeared, and now, I had no ability to breathe as her focus landed on me.

"Introduce us, Camilla," Lady Isolda snapped. "You must be from a local noble family, but I don't believe we've met."

Camilla suppressed a laugh behind one hand. "This is... Bellatrix. She's visiting family. We instantly became the best of friends, and I offered to show her around. I thought it would be fun to have a companion. Everyone at the castle is so unfriendly."

I swallowed my shock. In my gown, with my face plastered in makeup, Lady Isolda didn't recognize me. I inclined my head. "It's a pleasure to meet you. I've been hearing all about the village from Camilla."

"Which family are you connected to?" Lady Isolda asked.

"The Templeton-Masons," I said after a second of brain freeze. They were a minor noble family who lived on the village's periphery. They had an average-sized estate and kept out of the family's way, so I was confident Lady Isolda wouldn't know all members of that particular family.

It seemed to satisfy her curiosity, and she lost interest in me, returning her ice tundra gaze back to Camilla.

"Lady Isolda, my apologies, but we have a situation." Warwick slid in beside her.

"What is it?"

"We have identified a threat. Everyone needs to return to the castle."

I could have kissed him. Warwick had saved me from an extraordinarily dangerous situation.

"I don't have to go, do I?" Camilla asked. "I'm having such fun with my new friend."

"Of course you must come back to the castle. You're important to us. No complaints. This way." Lady Isolda gestured for Camilla to stand.

"What about Bellatrix?" Camilla asked.

"She can find her own way home." Lady Isolda hauled Camilla out of her seat and gripped her elbow. "Are those food stains on your gown?"

Camilla brushed at the silk.

"No matter. Warwick, lead the way." Lady Isolda didn't glance back at me as they hurried out of the tavern.

A few seconds later, Hodgepodge dropped from the rafters onto my shoulder with an audible thud. I slumped in my seat and leaned my head against his side. "Even though I don't usually drink, I need a stiff one after that encounter."

Evander Thorne slid into the seat Camilla had vacated. "You scrub up well, Bell."

"How long have you been here?" I asked.

He grinned. "Long enough. Warwick let me know what was going on. I thought you might need backup."

"I was beginning to think I would when Lady Isolda showed." I swirled my lemonade. "Is the threat fake?"

"Of course, but the family won't know that. Warwick is simply doing his job. Maybe he saw me as the threat." Evander winked. "Don't worry, we've got your back."

Hodgepodge licked my cheek. "You're wearing far too much blush. You don't look like you."

"For once, I'm happy about that. It saved me from Lady Isolda's scrutiny." I swiped my hands across my face. "I feel sorry for Camilla being stuck in that situation, but she's scary. All she wanted to talk about was how to murder Prince Jasper."

"You said nothing incriminating, did you?" Alarm flashed in Evander's eyes.

I shook my head. "She wasn't letting the subject go, though. She seems lonely."

"She also sounded insane," Hodgepodge said.

Evander nodded. "I agree. Stay as far away from her as possible. If she's talking about getting the prince murdered, you can't be associated with her."

I rested my head against the wall. "Have you any news about the stone heart amulet?"

"I'm still looking. Whoever's got it is still using it. More statues appeared in the park first thing this morning. They've already been moved."

"I didn't see any when I was there. I should check in the stone chamber. The new statues are probably in there by now."

Evander caught hold of my arm. "Before you go, you need to watch your back. Camilla's latched onto you for a reason, and it's not for anything good. She could be looking for someone to take the fall if she puts her insane, murderous plan into action."

"I'll do what I can to keep my distance, but I can't refuse her without getting in trouble."

"If she keeps talking about killing her fiancé, she'll be out of the picture soon enough." Evander released my arm, and his gaze ran over the dress. "You should keep that. It makes you look even cuter than usual."

I looked at the dress and shook my head. "I'll wear it for my next cleaning shift, shall I? I'll catch up with you later." I hurried away with Hodgepodge, tugging the red shawl tight around my shoulders. Everything felt so uncertain, and all I wanted to do was get back to my dragons and a quiet life. I had a feeling that wasn't happening anytime soon.

Chapter 15

I was back in my much more familiar, comfortable clothes, my face scrubbed of makeup as I headed to the chamber. It was just past five o'clock in the evening, and I was concerned what kind of mess the place would be in. Prince Jasper had said he'd arrange things, but I didn't trust him.

So, I was surprised and relieved to discover Maggie Buckleberry lurking in the servants' tunnel. She turned when she heard me approaching, throwing her arms up. "Thank the dragons you're here! This work is backbreaking. I'd never have agreed to do it if I'd had a choice, but I was ordered to do it. I don't even work for the family anymore, but Prince Jasper accosted me in the yard and insisted I help."

I briefly hugged her. "Thanks, Maggie. I was entertaining Camilla Oldsbrook. She insisted I show her around the village."

"Prince Jasper's bride-to-be?"

"I know. It's a long story, but she demanded I accompany her so, much like you, I had no choice. I'm just glad the dragons were left in your capable hands."

"You're welcome to have them back," she said. "I did my best, but the visitors are messy. Some of the offerings they leave verge on the inappropriate. I found three plastic dolls with no clothes on. Who'd leave something like that for the dragons, and what do they even mean? I can't imagine the dragons would be interested in a naked doll."

I laughed softly. "Visitors never cease to amaze me. Thanks again."

"You're welcome. I'm sure they'll be glad to have you back." Maggie glanced through the tiny crack in the door as visitors milled around. "Something's wrong with the chamber's heating system. You should get that looked at before someone complains."

"What makes you say that?"

"I was in there cleaning, and it got smoky. I thought it was my eyes playing tricks on me the first time, but it happened again. I smelled smoke, and when I looked around, I couldn't see anything odd. Have you noticed that happening when you've been in there?"

I gripped my hands behind my back. "How strange. I'll look into it."

"Maybe it was just me. I was so stressed I'd mess up that I started seeing things."

I longed to tell Maggie about Emberthorn and Stormwing coming back, but having been friendly with her for several years, I knew she was dreadful at keeping secrets. And this was one secret we had to keep until the dragons were ready to escape.

"Have you found a new job yet?" I asked her.

She pulled a face. "Nothing exciting. Gwit wants me to apprentice with him in the bottle-making factory, but I don't want to get my hands covered in burn marks. And he gets so sweaty working on the kilns. It's revolting. I've been helping a few days a week in the apothecary store. It'll do for now until I find something better."

"I'm glad you found work away from the castle," I said.

"I won't be coming back here soon. My experience with Prince Godric scarred me for life."

"I don't blame you."

She gave me a look, and it was full of questions. "We're all so grateful for everything you did for us. If it weren't for you, I don't think I'd be alive. You're our hero, Bell."

I blushed under her praise. "I'd do it again, although I'm hoping I won't have to."

"You don't have to worry about me getting into trouble again. Gwit's been making me train every day with my enchanted blade. I'm quite the knife thrower these days." Maggie mimed slinging a blade through the air. She kissed my cheek. "I'd better go. My brother will worry about where I am. If I'm even five minutes late these days, he wants to send out a search party. See you soon. You'll have to come for cake when you have a day off."

I bid her goodbye, then waited by the door, watching the visitors. Although, more accurately, I was watching for smoke. I was glad when the last visitor left, so I could dash into the chamber.

My eyes hadn't deceived me. Stormwing was smoking!

I hurried over to him. His statue portrayed him rearing up, so I could only ever touch his back claws or the lower part of his stone belly and tail to get his attention.

I gave him a formal bow, curtsied, and held out my hand. "You may not realize you're doing this, but you're smoking. And people are noticing."

"Stormwing has been in a foul mood all day," Emberthorn said from his crouched position. "Nothing I say placates him."

"Stop your huffing and puffing, you oversized beastie," Hodgepodge snapped at Stormwing. "If you give us away, you'll never get out of here, and Bell will be tossed into the dungeon."

"I'll huff and puff all over you if you speak to me so disrespectfully again."

I jumped back. It was the first time I'd heard Stormwing speak, his voice a scratchy growl.

Emberthorn rumbled a laugh. "His physical voice came back early this morning. We were planning on telling you, but then Camilla interfered with our plans. Stormwing is grouchy because she spoiled his surprise."

I grinned up at Stormwing. "That's amazing news. It means you're getting stronger. You'll both be able to leave soon."

"No one will leave if this smoking buffoon doesn't put a cap on it," Hodgepodge said.

"I'll smoke you like a slab of ham if you keep talking." Stormwing spoke with a voice full of gravel and grit, as if his throat were still made of stone.

"Let's be respectful to the enormous grumpy dragon," I murmured to Hodgepodge.

"He should be grateful to us," Hodgepodge said. "You break your back every day to keep them happy, and the first word Stormwing says is a complaint."

"You'd complain too if you'd spent years trapped in stone, tiny lizard."

I gently rested a hand on one of Stormwing's claws. "It must be difficult, but we're so close to getting you out. Just hold the smoke and the grumbling for a little longer, and then you'll be free to stamp and snarl as much as you like. Won't that be fun?"

"I want to be free now! I have so much fire to breathe, and I intend to pour it over the Ithric family."

"We've discussed this," Emberthorn said. "No attacking the family until we have a solid plan. And once we're out, we'll have more healing to do."

"I'm strong enough to whip that family into submission. It's no less than they deserve."

I gently cleared my throat as I got to work. "I don't disagree that they've done you great harm, but going after them with no plan is unwise. And you are far from an unwise dragon, Stormwing."

"Unless all those years trapped in stone have addled his brain," Hodgepodge said. "Show Bell respect. She is your emissary. You picked her."

Stormwing grumbled to himself, and the floor shook.

"That's enough, brother," Emberthorn said. "We know Bell is right for us. When she puts her foot down, we must listen to her. She is our voice of wisdom and reason."

I failed to hide my surprise. The dragons were much older and wiser than me.

Emberthorn laughed again. "Still doubting yourself, I see. There'll soon be no time left for that."

"I'm a work in progress." I swept up dirt and set aside the last of the offerings. "Settle yourself, Stormwing. I'll speak to Seraphina about when exactly we can move you."

"Don't trust her," Stormwing said. "Not after everything she did."

"Look at what she's doing for you now. She's barely sleeping and is determined to fix her wrongs."

"It'll take more than a little sleep deprivation to repair the damage of her deceit." Stormwing growled again.

I finished sweeping then counted the stone statues and discovered five new ones had appeared. My hand shook as I touched the familiar face of a villager. "Whoever is doing this is out of control. No one is safe."

"And it'll only get worse," Emberthorn said. "If someone is using the stone heart amulet, the magic it contains is addictive. The person wielding it will barely know what they're doing by now. The amulet's power has taken control. It grows stronger the more it is used."

"Which makes it even more dangerous," Hodgepodge said. "Bell should stay away from this mystery."

I checked the time. "We'll discuss this later. The doors are about to open. Stormwing, please, no more smoke."

The floor shook. "I'll do what I can."

I dashed away and hid in the tunnel again, my gaze fixed on Stormwing. I could tell he was trying, but there was still a cloud of smoke around his head. If anyone looked closely, they'd discover his secret. And if the royal family were alerted, this would all be over.

The visitor session was almost at an end when a small boy of around eight pointed up at Stormwing. "He's smoking! Mama, look! The dragon is smoking."

I froze, one hand on the door. I could see smoke, too. Stormwing was struggling to keep his composure.

"I have to go out there," I whispered to Hodgepodge. "I'll make an excuse and say there's a problem with the ventilation system."

"There's no need. Backup is here." Hodgepodge was peering through the gap.

I focused on the crowd of visitors and spotted Astrid striding toward the family, staring up at Stormwing. She was puffing on an enormous pipe, creating a billow of smoke around her. When she got close enough, she inhaled deeply and breathed smoke all over them.

The mother coughed and waved a hand across her face, tucking her son behind her.

Astrid grinned and puffed some more. "Sorry. It's a filthy habit, but I can't seem to break it."

The child's mother looked at her in disapproval. She took hold of the boy's hand and headed to the door as he whined and pointed back at Stormwing.

Astrid watched them go, smirking as she puffed on the pipe that hung out of the corner of her mouth. She glanced my way and winked before striding around Stormwing, creating billows of smoke all around him that drifted slowly to the ceiling.

I leaned against the wall and closed my eyes for a few seconds. That was too close. If Astrid hadn't been so quick, Stormwing would have been exposed, and everything we'd worked so hard to achieve would be finished.

"We're running out of time," I said. "Hodgepodge, go find everyone. Tell them to meet at our place just after midnight. We need action. We have to get the dragons out."

"Seraphina, too?" Hodgepodge was already scuttling along the corridor.

I nodded. "If you can. She's been reluctant to leave her room recently, other than to come to the chamber and spend time with the dragons. If she won't visit, make sure she tells you exactly how soon we can move them."

"I'll make sure everybody is there." Hodgepodge dashed away.

I peeked through the gap, happy to see the last of the visitors leaving. Astrid had also gone. For now, the dragons had to be my focus. Then I'd deal with the maniac turning everybody to stone.

Chapter 16

Having finished a busy afternoon working in the castle, I wanted to lounge with my feet up, snuggled under a cozy blanket with Hodgepodge, and eat my own weight in homemade cookies. But, alas, there were dragons to rescue and a crazed amulet-wielding killer to deal with, so my dreams of a quiet night in would have to wait.

I hurried back to my lodgings, Hodgepodge on my shoulder. "Everyone agreed to meet us?"

"They said they would be here. Although Seraphina was acting strangely. She kept scratching herself and stamping around in a terrible temper when I spoke to her about the plan."

"The exhaustion is getting to her. She feels so guilty because of what she did to the dragons that she's punishing herself."

"So she should. I stand by my original comment. It's a disgrace how she mistreated the dragons because she had a fight with her family and wanted to prove a point," Hodgepodge said.

"We all make mistakes when we're young. Some of us also make mistakes when we're not so young." I opened the door to my lodgings. Evander, Griffin, and Astrid were inside, having made themselves comfortable on my sparse furnishings.

"I made supper." Griffin strode into the kitchen. "I was waiting for you before serving."

"I'm too nervous to eat," I said, but the bowl of stew he pressed on me after I'd taken off my cloak overcame my nerves.

"Let's get started, shall we?" Astrid said. "I've got places to go and people to rob."

"We're waiting for two others," I said.

A second later, there was a light tap on the door. I opened it, and Warwick and Seraphina stood outside. I ushered them in.

"We're still trusting this guy?" Astrid jabbed a finger at Warwick.

"After the help he provided when we rescued the women, of course, we trust him," I said.

"Could be he's playing the long game." Evander glared at Warwick as he slurped up stew. "He's lulling us into a false sense of security before turning us over to the family and getting a reward."

"The bounty on your head doesn't make it worth my effort." Warwick bared his teeth at Evander in a twisted version of a smile. "And I'm helping Bell, not you. And the dragons. They're my focus."

I touched Seraphina's arm where she'd been scratching. "Is everything okay?"

She hid her hands behind her back. "It's my own fault. I got the potion I've been using on Stormwing and Emberthorn on my skin, and I can't stop scratching."

Seraphina looked wretched. Even more wretched than the last time I saw her. I gently squeezed her elbow.

"This will soon be over. Why not give everyone an update? We need a timeline to know when we can move the dragons. Now Stormwing is smoking, we don't have long left."

Her nod was jerky as her gaze darted around the room, not settling on anything for more than a fraction of a second. "If everyone is available, we can move them tonight. The hideout is ready, and I believe they're strong enough to fly."

Everyone stilled. We exchanged glances, and a ripple of excitement passed through the room.

"It's finally happening," Evander said. "After all these years of wondering if we'd ever see a dragon free in our realm again, we're doing it!"

"Which is good." I stamped on my nervous excitement. "Stormwing has been blowing smoke on and off all day. Astrid covered for him, but we're out of time. If we don't move them now, a member of the family will figure out what's going on and destroy them."

"What's the plan?" Evander asked. "You know the dragons best, so how should we move them?"

I looked at Seraphina for answers, but she shook her head. "I've done all I can. The release magic activated because of your blood connection. You have the most direct link to Emberthorn and Stormwing."

"You really think they're strong enough to fly?" I asked.

"Not fast, but they'll be able to travel a fair distance before exhaustion overtakes them. It won't be elegant, though. They haven't used their wings in over two decades, so it'll be a bumpy flight."

I took a moment to get my thoughts in order. "We need to distract the castle guards. Something big and flashy to keep them away from the chamber while we set the dragons loose."

"That'll be our department." Evander grinned at Astrid. "We'll make something go boom."

"Nothing important needs to go boom, though, and I don't want anyone getting hurt," I said.

"Leave it to us," Astrid said. "We'll give the guards a night they'll never forget."

"The last of the magic trapping Emberthorn and Stormwing will also need to be removed." I focused on Seraphina. "Can you do that?"

"I'll need assistance, but I can manage it."

I looked at Griffin, and he nodded.

"You two are together, then," I said. "We'll go in as a team. Evander and Astrid, you fix the distraction. We'll wait for a sign before releasing Emberthorn and Stormwing."

"The sign will be when there's an enormous explosion," Astrid said. "You won't miss it."

"Seraphina and Griffin, you go to the stone chamber with the last of the release magic prepared," I said.

"It's in potion form and will need to be sprinkled over them." Seraphina glanced at Griffin. "I'll tackle Stormwing, and you look after Emberthorn."

"I can do that," Griffin said. "What about you, Bell? Will you need to be with the dragons when they're released?"

"I'll be close. I'll stick with Warwick. We need to keep a low profile since we can't afford for Warwick to be discovered helping us."

Evander chuckled. "Got the ladies protecting you now, have you, Warwick?"

"It's not that!" I said. "Warwick is a valuable inside asset. He has access to private conversations none of us could ever hope to hear. We can't risk him being discovered helping us. The family would destroy him."

"They could try to destroy me," Warwick grumbled, "although I appreciate not being thrown into the thick of things."

"Neither of us can be seen," I said. "If the royal family discovers we're involved, we'll spend the rest of our very short lives on the run."

"Sure, sure. And I definitely don't want that for you, Bell." Evander flashed a wicked smile at Warwick.

"We'll watch the entrances and make sure no one comes in to disturb you," I said to Griffin and Seraphina. "Hodgepodge, you go with Astrid and Evander."

He shook his head. "I'm staying with you. I don't like doing this, and I definitely don't like doing it if I'm not perched on your shoulder."

I kissed his scaled side. "We'll only be apart for a short time. Once Evander and Astrid are ready to go, you run back and join us in the chamber. Once you're there, we'll release the dragons and get out."

He grumbled to himself then nodded.

I looked around the group, my heart thumping out a rhythm of excitement and panic. "We're really doing this."

"You bet your sweet cheeks we are." Evander stood. "Let's go cause destruction."

I held up a hand. "Wait! Before everyone goes, I want to thank you. I couldn't have done this without you."

"This is all down to you," Astrid said. "If you hadn't angered Prince Godric enough to whack you, your blood would never have ended up on Emberthorn. The dragons would still be stuck in stone, and we'd be none the wiser."

The group nodded as a one, united in their quest to see this mission to the end.

"And the dragons chose you as their emissary," Seraphina said. "They always pick wisely. It takes great heart and spirit to support the dragons."

"All I've ever done is clean for them," I said.

"You've done much more than that," Griffin said. "You never stopped loving them. And you always believed in them when everyone else gave up hope. Loyalty carries weight with dragons."

"We're on the brink of change, and the family will realize how much is changing when Emberthorn and Stormwing are free." Evander chuckled. "Let's move, Astrid. I'm longing to destroy something and ruin the family's quiet night."

They slid into the gloom of just past midnight, Hodgepodge unhappily perched on Astrid's shoulder. I waited a few tense minutes with Griffin, Warwick, and Seraphina before we left my lodgings and hurried into the darkness. Bulky clouds scudded across the sky, blotting out the crescent moon and making it easy for us to walk among the shadows and draw no attention from castle patrols.

We had to pause several times as guards appeared by the main gate, but we were soon by the side of the castle, slipping past stone walls toward the servants' entrance. We dashed along the tunnel, no one speaking, our footsteps rapid and sure, matching my racing heartbeat. Nothing could go wrong. This would be our only chance to get the dragons free.

There was a soft buzzing in my ears that made me slow.

"This isn't the time to doubt yourself, Bell." It was Emberthorn! "We trust you, so trust yourself. You have your companions around you, and we're working together for the same thing."

"Is anyone else hearing that?" I whispered.

"What are you hearing?" Warwick asked.

"Most likely Emberthorn," Seraphina said, her disembodied voice behind me. "He's been ready to go for weeks but has refused to move because Stormwing wasn't strong enough."

"They will always be loyal to each other," Warwick said. "When they ruled, they were a perfect balance of strength and solidarity. Emberthorn calmed Stormwing's tornado, and Stormwing got Emberthorn moving when he could be lackadaisical."

"Tell your companion I heard that," Emberthorn said with a chuckle. "He's not wrong. My brother and I rule well together. We hope to do that again soon."

We reached the door that led into the stone chamber, and I pushed it open. The room was silent. The lights were off, and only the intermittent glow from the moon illuminated the room. I took a moment to look around, even though I was certain the place would be empty at this time of night.

"It's all clear," I whispered to the others.

We hurried out as a group, and I left the tunnel door open so Hodgepodge could get in. Warwick patrolled around the circular edge of the chamber before seeming convinced there were no threats. There were, however, more stone statues. He stationed himself by the main entrance, and I took the other door. Seraphina and Griffin conferred for a moment before she passed him a glass jar of amber liquid.

"Are you excited?" I directed the question to Emberthorn, sensing his anticipation.

"It will be a joy to stretch my wings and roar my flame," he said.

"I just want to breathe fire." Stormwing's abruptly growly voice in my head made me jump.

Smoke billowed from Emberthorn's nostrils. "We're learning new skills every day. Now, I must focus. The last part of this release spell will be intense."

I could do nothing but wait by the door, listening intently for signs of approaching footsteps.

Seraphina stood in front of Stormwing, while Griffin waited by Emberthorn. As the seconds ticked by, my anxiety grew. What if someone had caught Evander and Astrid? Or Hodgepodge? We wouldn't know if it was okay to cast the final release magic.

"He's on his way. Your scaled companion has never let you down, and he's not about to start now," Emberthorn said.

Only when I saw Hodgepodge launch himself out of the servants' tunnel and dash toward me, did I relax. "Is everything good?"

"We're all set. Let's get these dragons free." He leaped onto my shoulder and nuzzled his scaled face against mine.

Seraphina and Griffin went to work, sprinkling the potion over the dragons. With every sprinkle, steam rose. It grew so intense that the room became as hot as a sauna, and sweat dripped down my face.

Hodgepodge delighted in the change in temperature and flicked out his leathery neck ruff. "This is the kind of climate I was meant for. Not the cold drear of this place."

"Once the dragons get free, we'll see more sunshine," I whispered. "You can sun puddle bathe for hours."

The steam grew more intense, and a hot wind gusted through the chamber, swirling around us. I peered at the dragons. Seraphina and Griffin kept running around them, sprinkling more release magic. It got hotter and hotter, and the air shimmered with a haze of heat.

"Any second now," Seraphina said. "Get ready. Their stone could shatter, so stay out of the blast zone."

"What blast zone?" Hodgepodge dug his claws into my shoulder. "This whole place is a blast zone."

His last words were whipped away as the wind reached a crescendo of chaos, and there was a loud snap. Rather than the stone flying everywhere, it dropped off the dragons and crashed to the floor.

I stared openmouthed, my pulse pounding and my smile burning so big it hurt my face. Emberthorn pulsed, his intense green scales on full display. Stormwing's scales were a dull red, with black tips. He was the first to move and crashed to the floor. He lay there for a few seconds then opened his eyes and bit Seraphina.

Chapter 17

It took me a few seconds to realize what had happened, but my eyes hadn't deceived me. Seraphina lay between Stormwing's enormous jaws, and she wasn't moving.

I raced over, Hodgepodge clinging to my shoulder. "Seraphina is a friend! Don't hurt her."

Stormwing growled, and smoke billowed around him.

"Stop it! She helped to get you free. Stormwing, let her go." My heart ricocheted against my ribs. Had Stormwing been driven mad by his long confinement?

Emberthorn took a few faltering steps toward us but lost his balance and hit the floor. "Calm yourself, brother. And spit out Seraphina before you damage her frail form."

Stormwing growled low in his throat then did as his brother instructed. Seraphina tumbled to the floor, rolling over several times. She was soggy but appeared unharmed.

"She's a traitor," Stormwing said. "I feel sick just looking at her."

"Shush. Enough of that. Seraphina knows she's wronged you, but she's made amends. You wouldn't be free if it weren't for her dedication." I helped Seraphina up, and although she was wobbly on her knees, she was intact.

"It's fine. I expected nothing less," she said.

"You should apologize," I said to Stormwing.

The amber in Stormwing's eyes darkened. "And you should apologize for not properly greeting me."

I hesitated. In the heat of the moment, I'd forgotten myself. Dragons were formal creatures, and offering the wrong greeting put you in their bad books for years.

I began the formal greeting, but Emberthorn nudged me from behind, almost knocking me off my feet. "Ignore him. He is being unreasonable. And we have no time for formalities."

Stormwing growled several times before nodding.

"Is everyone ready to move?" I asked.

"What would you have us do?" Emberthorn asked.

Griffin and Warwick stood together. I was with Seraphina and Hodgepodge. This was the part of the plan I'd hoped would work but hadn't been able to test. "The easiest way out is up. You need to fly through the glass roof."

The dragons examined the roof and had a silent conversation between themselves, staring, blinking, and grumbling.

"We are ready." Emberthorn grabbed me, Hodgepodge, and Warwick in his mouth and tossed us onto his back. Then he coiled and torpedoed up, moving so fast I almost fell before he smashed through the glass.

The breaking wood and falling glass drowned out our combined cries of protest. I was positioned behind Warwick and clung to his back, Emberthorn's raised scales acting as a kind of saddle. Hodgepodge was squashed between the two of us.

Emberthorn had curled one giant wing over us as a shield as he'd blasted out of the glass, but that movement tipped him off balance, and he flipped several times before righting himself. I pressed my knees against Emberthorn and closed my eyes. I didn't open them again until the world stopped spinning and my stomach caught up with me.

"Hodgepodge, you okay?" It was freezing as Emberthorn clumsily flew through the night. Despite being seated behind Warwick, I was being buffeted by icy blasts of wind. Warwick must have been getting a lot worse since he had no shield, but I hadn't heard him complain.

"It's not the ride I'd have chosen," Hodgepodge said, "but we're free! And Stormwing is behind us."

I risked a glance over my shoulder and regretted it as the world spun again and my stomach danced a fast-paced samba, threatening to scramble up my throat and launch into the sky. Stormwing was behind us, and he carried Seraphina and Griffin on his back. In the distance, a huge fire blazed in the castle. Whatever Evander and Astrid had done, it had worked.

"My apologies for the less than elegant departure," Emberthorn said. "I needed as much speed as possible. Otherwise, the roof wouldn't have shattered. Vertical takeoff doesn't come naturally to dragons, so it was hit and miss it would work."

"I'm glad it did," I yelled over the wind. "Otherwise, we'd have had to smash through stone walls, and that would have drawn too much attention." I shivered in my scaled seat and clung to Warwick. "Everything good up front?"

"I'm having the time of my life," he grumbled. "Did I ever tell you I loathe flying?"

"If it's always like this, I can understand why," I said. "It's not what I expected from my first dragon flight. Well, I've never really thought about flying on the back of a dragon. It's unusual."

"Many, many years ago, hundreds, in fact, dragons had riders," Emberthorn said, his wings moving erratically as he fought to keep balance. "They trained together and were bonded for life. Riders were gifted extra-long life and enjoyed the privileges of being within the dragon community. It was a highly prized position."

"You're talking about the Great Dragon War?" I asked. "You were there?"

"No, I was a youngster when the war began, so I was never gifted a rider, but I was always happy to be ridden for pleasure rather than in combat. My family fought in the wars. The tradition died out when the battles ceased, and slowly, people stopped riding us. I miss the company. And I assure you, when I have my skills back and my strength returns, the flight is smooth and warm. I have been still for so long that my thermal regulation is malfunctioning. That is why you feel so cold."

"I can help with that," Hodgepodge said. "Well, not you. Sorry, Emberthorn. Give me a minute."

"What are you doing?" I asked.

"Becoming your hot water bottle. It's a trick I learned since being able to go super-size."

Hodgepodge leaned against me, and he grew warm.

"Wow! You're full of surprises." I wrapped a frozen hand around his belly.

"I can't do it for long, but it'll take the edge off until we land."

I snuggled closer to Warwick so he'd get the benefit of Hodgepodge's warmth too, and the flight became more comfortable. It was shaky, though, and from the occasional scream I heard behind us, Stormwing was also struggling with his flying abilities. Or maybe he was misbehaving to scare Seraphina.

"Keep heading toward the trees," I said to Emberthorn. "You'll sense a protective magic barrier we've put around your hideout."

"I can already sense it. And I'll be glad to land."

"I'll be glad when you land too," Warwick said.

I closed my eyes for a few seconds and took several deep breaths. A smile hit me, and it wouldn't stop growing. We'd done it. The dragons were free. Finally, the realm had its dragons back where they belonged.

Emberthorn kept flying, but his movements grew increasingly sluggish, and he was losing height at an alarming rate.

"Not much farther. Keep going. You've got this. When we get to your hideout, there's food and a safe place to sleep," I encouraged him as the ground came into view too fast for my liking.

"I would like to sleep for half a year," he said.

"We may not be able to afford you that," Warwick said. "You and your brother are free, but the Ithric family will soon be hunting you."

"One step at a time," I said. "We get the dragons tucked away, and we figure out what to do about the family."

The descent was clunky, and Emberthorn struggled as he slid through the magic and skimmed over the trees, branches snapping as he whacked into them.

"There's a clearing up ahead. Land there," I said.

Emberthorn grunted a reply, his wings quivering.

"Hold on," Warwick said. "The landing will be as rough as the departure."

I gripped him tight, my legs shaking from the effort of holding on so fiercely. Emberthorn dipped, pulling back his wings to slow his speed, and landed. He almost made it, but at the last second, he lost his balance, tipped over, and we spilled off his back and rolled into spiky bushes.

"Look out below!" Griffin yelled. "We've got an angry, exhausted dragon coming in with no ability to fly or steer."

"I'll bite your head off for that comment," Stormwing yelled back. "Clear a path!"

Emberthorn rolled onto his side and curled his wings around himself. I grabbed Hodgepodge and used a tree as cover, while Warwick curled against a boulder, as Stormwing crashed onto his belly. His wings remained splayed as he lay there, deep breathing.

Seraphina and Griffin rolled off him, checking they were still in one piece. Amazingly, they were.

Astrid and Evander appeared from the trees and ran over to join us. We stood around the exhausted dragons, huge grins on our faces.

"We pulled it off," Evander said, shaking his head but still smiling.

"You didn't doubt me for a second, did you?" I asked. "I knew exactly what was going on."

He nudged me. "I had one or two tiny doubts."

"I thought the dragons would crash and burn." Astrid peered at Emberthorn with amazement in her eyes. "We've been following you from the castle."

"We will always protect our emissary," Emberthorn grumbled out.

I headed to Seraphina, who had separated herself from the group. "How are you doing? It must have been a shock when Stormwing grabbed you."

"That's a matter for another time," Emberthorn said, still on the ground, taking it all in but not moving. "We have complicated issues to work through with Seraphina, but we can manage that on our own when there are fewer pressing matters facing us."

Seraphina nodded. "Agreed."

We gathered around Emberthorn and waited for him to speak. He remained silent. It looked like he'd fallen asleep.

I cleared my throat. "Do you mean the Ithric family?"

Emberthorn's eyes jerked open. "My apologies. I meant our most immediate threat needs to be stopped."

"We've worked hard on the protection magic in this area. And we're the only ones who can see the location thanks to shielding magic. Everyone else will pass by and have no idea you're here," I said.

"And we appreciate that, but now we're free, you must focus on finding the stone killer. We would help, but..." He lifted a limp wing.

"You're too weak to do anything after that flight," Seraphina said. "You must stay hidden until you've recovered."

"We intend to. But with the stone heart amulet being recklessly used, no one is truly safe," Emberthorn said.

"There is something darkly unnatural about that power. I still believe there is dragon magic mixed in with the amulet's power. If I'm right, it means we have a rogue dragon to deal with."

Seraphina dipped her chin. "We would know if there was such a creature in the realm."

"You doubt my brother's word?" Stormwing snarled but made no move toward Seraphina.

She shied away from him. "Of course not. But a dragon would have been seen and reported to the family."

"You must deal with whoever has the amulet," Emberthorn said. "They're out of control, and the magic has captured them. They're dangerous to all, even us, while we're weakened."

"I can defeat them." Stormwing staggered to his feet but rocked to one side, almost stamping on me.

"Keep your clumsy claws away from Bell!" Hodgepodge launched off my shoulder, and in midair, he transformed, growing to his enormous, beautiful size. He stared down Stormwing and growled in his face.

"It's okay! Stormwing didn't mean it." I raced toward them, still not used to seeing Hodgepodge go super-sized.

"I will not have you stamped on by some clumsy, angry dragon with an attitude problem." Hodgepodge growled again. "No one will harm you."

Stormwing stared at Hodgepodge, his mouth agape. Then he lifted his head and growled out a gravel-filled laugh. "Here is an ally we can rely on. Not these untrustworthy, deceitful humans."

"Hey! We're helping you." I stepped onto Hodgepodge's front foot and hugged it. "We've done nothing but help ever since we figured out we could get you free."

"Apologize to Bell," Hodgepodge said.

"Brother, your bad mood is getting the better of you," Emberthorn said. "Bell is our emissary. You must treat her with the respect she deserves."

Stormwing lowered his head and growled to himself. "My apologies. I'll admit, Bell isn't awful."

"Bell is excellent," Emberthorn said. "She will protect us. For now, she must focus on eliminating the stone killer and restoring the statues. Our quest will wait until we are strong enough to pursue our rightful place as rulers."

"I can do that." I glanced at my friends.

"We're all here to support you, Bell," Warwick said. "We've got the dragons covered. If they want you to focus on who's turning everyone to stone, it needs to be your priority."

I rested a hand against Hodgepodge and looked around at my strangely wonderful extended family. "Well, okay then. Let's go solve this mystery."

Chapter 18

"Play things cool," Hodgepodge whispered as I strode toward the castle the next morning. "We know nothing, we saw nothing, and we're only here to clean."

I nodded. After our late-night flee with the dragons, everything felt different, but I had to behave as if I knew nothing about their escape. And when I approached the main castle entrance, it seemed as if it was business as normal. There were the usual guards outside, who barely nodded at me as I passed, and the typical hustle and bustle within the inner circle of the castle walls.

"The family must know what has happened in the stone chamber by now," I whispered.

"If they do, they're keeping things under wraps because they don't want anyone knowing the dragons are back."

"They want to destroy them before anyone finds out they're free." I gritted my teeth as I hurried along the main corridor and grabbed my cleaning equipment. I just had to play it cool for a little longer, just until the dragons were back to full strength. Then it wouldn't matter if anyone from the Ithric family knew I'd been involved, because Emberthorn and Stormwing would protect me.

My hopes of an easy start to the day faded as I approached the stone chamber to discover Lady Isolda and Prince Jasper standing outside, conferring with several guards. I hung back, hoping they'd leave, but they remained in deep conversation, although Prince Jasper kept yawning and looking around, suggesting he wanted to be anywhere else.

"You have a right to be here." Hodgepodge had slid onto my back, so he was out of sight. "Walk over as if you're about to start work, same as usual. You don't want to make them suspicious by lurking in the shadows."

I waited until Hodgepodge had settled inside the large pocket of my underskirt before cautiously approaching the group. No one paid me any attention. It wasn't until I attempted to slide past a guard that I was stopped.

"You can't go inside," he said. "There's been an incident."

"Oh! I was just... I need to set up the chamber for the visitors. Have more statues arrived?" I asked as innocently as possible.

Lady Isolda spared me no glance as she turned and strode away with Prince Jasper beside her.

"Does that mean I should go in?" I asked one of the guards.

"We'll be late opening today," he said. "The dragons have been taken away for... repairs."

"They've been damaged?"

"That's not your business. We won't be opening until noon. Orders from the family. Come back then."

I longed to ask more questions about the damage to the roof and how they'd moved two enormous stone dragons out of the chamber without smashing a wall down, but the fewer questions I asked, the better. I turned and scurried away, my heart racing at twice the speed of my feet.

Once I'd stowed my cleaning equipment, I leaned against the wall and took several deep breaths until I felt calmer. When I opened my eyes, Griffin was walking toward me. He raised his hand in greeting.

I hurried to meet him. "Have you seen what they're doing in the stone chamber?"

He nodded, pressed a finger to his lips, and ushered me outside and into an empty stable that smelled of fresh hay and hot horse. "When I got back here last night, it was chaos. Lady Isolda was screeching and ordering guards around. Everyone was in fear for their lives."

"I just saw her. She seems composed now. One of the guards told me the dragons have been taken for repair."

Griffin nodded. "It's the cover story they must be using. They need to hide the fact the dragons are on the loose for as long as possible, because the second people know, the family's grip on control will slip."

"Have you heard from the others?" I asked.

"Nothing. When I finish my shift at noon today, I'm off to the forest." He raised his eyebrows.

"I hope our new friends had a comfortable night," I said. "I barely slept thinking about what we've achieved."

"They'll be fine. And our new friends want you to focus on figuring out who is misusing the stone heart amulet, not on them."

"I haven't forgotten," I said. "Now I have my morning free, I can poke around."

"You can do better than that. I know Augustus's wife, Jenny. She's still in the house he was gifted when Augustus worked at the castle."

"Introduce me to her!" I said.

"If the scorned wife is turning people to stone, we go nowhere near her." Hodgepodge scrambled out of my skirt pocket and onto my shoulder.

Griffin checked the time. "Jenny is an early riser, so she should be up. Let's get breakfast to take with us, and we can ask a few discreet questions about Augustus. She must be wondering what happened to him."

"That's if she didn't kill him." I left the stable, and we hurried toward the market. "If Jenny is innocent, she won't know Augustus was turned to stone and then broken into a thousand pieces."

"We need to be careful when we question her," Griffin said.

"Or not at all. A scorned wife is always a dangerous one," Hodgepodge said. "We should take the morning off and catch up on sleep and read that book about fairies you've been meaning to start."

That sounded tempting, but I couldn't let the dragons down.

"Jenny has influence. Her role as Augustus's wife got her on several committees run by the family. If she grows suspicious of us, we'll be in trouble," Griffin said.

"Let's see just how dangerous she is before making assumptions," I replied.

We stopped by a bakery stall, and Griffin ordered half a dozen fruit scones. He led the way through the market, past the cheap quarter where my lodgings were located, and up a short hill until we reached an affluent area of the village, with stunning views over the fields.

He stopped and tapped on an ornately carved wooden door.

"How do you know Jenny?" I asked him.

"From basket weaving."

"You weave?"

He shrugged. "I like to keep busy. Jenny is into arts and crafts, and we met on an evening course. She's got talent. She does sewing, basket weaving, wreath making. She's always got some project on the go."

The door inched open, and a short, plump woman of around fifty with iron-gray hair peered out at us. "Oh! Griffin. This is a surprise. Was I expecting you?"

"I hope you don't mind the early alarm call," he said. "I brought breakfast. This is my friend Bell and her companion, Hodgepodge."

Jenny nodded a greeting as she opened the door wider. "You know me. Always up with the lark. And scones! My favorite. Please, come in." She wore fluffy slippers with bobbles on the big toes and an oversized dressing gown in a charming shade of blue. "You know where the kitchen is. Be a dear and brew the tea while I make myself more presentable."

"You've been here before?" I followed Griffin into a spacious open-plan kitchen, four times the size of my entire quarters.

"Jenny sometimes hosts the weaving classes here." Griffin set down the scones and moved competently around the kitchen, boiling water, and setting out cups and plates. "The ladies take it in turn to host. I'd do the same, but my place isn't exactly luxurious, and I can never get the stink of horse out of my rugs."

Jenny walked in a moment later in a smart purple tunic and matching skirt, her hair twisted off her face into a loose bun, grey tendrils around her cheekbones. "So, what brings you here?"

Griffin glanced at me.

"It's my fault," I said. "I work in the castle as a cleaner. I saw your husband, the stone statue version of him, recently, and learned Griffin knew you."

"Augustus has had a statue made of himself?" Jenny perched on a high stool and took a scone. "He didn't tell me."

"The likeness was remarkable," I said. "Unfortunately, the statue got destroyed. I found it when I opened the chamber to clean."

"That's unfortunate." Jenny broke off a piece of scone and popped it into her mouth.

"Yes. I hope Augustus wasn't too angry. It couldn't have been cheap to make."

"I wouldn't know about that. I haven't seen him for days."

"Oh! Is that unusual?"

"No. His work takes him all over the realm. He's often gone for weeks at a time on urgent business. Honestly, I have no interest in his work, so I leave him to do his thing. He always comes back, eventually."

He wouldn't this time, but it wasn't up to me to break the news to her.

Jenny smiled. "The scones are delicious, Griffin. Thank you for the treat."

"I got them from your favorite stall in the market."
He poured tea for us all. "And I'm glad we came. I don't
like to think of you alone."

"I'm more than content with my own company. And
of course, I have you and the others to entertain
me when Augustus is gone. I'm so looking forward
to my sewing circle later today. Are you sure I can't
encourage you to join us there, too? Several of my
ladies always ask after my handsome stable hand
friend."

Griffin shook his head, his cheeks glowing. "I'll stick
to the basket weaving."

"At least come to wreath making. It'll be our focus
until the royal wedding," Jenny said.

"You're making wreaths for the wedding?" I asked.

"Yes! Prince Jasper commissioned a hundred
wreaths. I almost fell off my seat when he placed the
order. I told him we weren't professionals, but he said
his bride wanted a rustic look and demanded wreaths.
Who was I to deny a prince? We've been working on
them every night into the small hours since he visited."

"Every night?" I asked.

"Yes. There are ten of us regulars who meet. I
always hold the wreath-making classes here. Would
you like to join us, Bell? We always need more nimble
hands. We start around eight o'clock in the evening
and go until our fingers tell us to stop." Jenny chuckled
and flexed her thin fingers. "Sometimes, we're still
here until dawn. Although, I think some of the ladies
stay that late for the free food and delicious wine."

"You do serve excellent wine," Griffin said. "Perhaps
I'll drop by and see if wreath-making is for me."

"It's addictive. And such fun," Jenny said. "Both of you must come. I'm rather glad Augustus isn't around because he'd only get in the way. He's not at all artistic. Always looking at figures and boring reports. Although, don't tell him I said that. He takes his work so seriously."

"Do you mind if I use your restroom?" I asked.

"Of course. Along the corridor, up the stairs, and it's the second door on your left. You can't miss it."

I left Jenny and Griffin chatting about wreaths and walked along the corridor. I checked into each room as I went.

"Do you notice something strange?" I whispered to Hodgepodge.

"I noticed I haven't been offered any scone to eat."

I chuckled softly. "You'll get some. Look around. This place has no sign of a man living in it. And there's not a single picture of Augustus anywhere."

Hodgepodge peered about as I headed up the stairs. "You're right. No pictures of him on the walls, just lots of handmade craft things dotted around."

"No men's shoes or slippers tucked under chairs," I said. "Let's check the bedrooms."

"Be quick. We don't want Jenny to catch you if she's wearing the stone heart amulet."

"From the way she's talking, she has no clue about Augustus's indiscretions. She seems happy if he stays out of her way, though. Some couples are like that. They've been together for such a long time that it's more of a convenient arrangement than a marriage. They live separate lives, coming together at appropriate times to put on a front. I imagine a man in Augustus's position would need a respectable wife on his arm when attending social functions."

"Jenny seems respectable and sane," Hodgepodge said. "And I imagine she has excellent taste in scones, if ever I get to try one."

A swift examination of the three bedrooms revealed not a scrap of evidence that anyone other than Jenny lived there. The restroom was the same. All the cabinets were full of fragrances, scented body lotions, and makeup.

"Some of this stuff could belong to Augustus," Hodgepodge said. "Maybe he enjoyed dressing up and smelling floral on his days off."

"Discount nothing." I eased the door shut and flushed the toilet before hurrying back down the stairs and joining Griffin and Jenny.

They were still chatting about wreath-making, and from everything Jenny was saying, she still thought Augustus was on a business trip. Although I had a feeling, when she learned the truth about him, she wouldn't be unhappy.

"Thank you for the tea," Griffin said. "We should leave. You must have a busy day ahead of you."

"Of course. What a delight you both stopped by." Jenny smiled warmly at me. "And it's always nice to meet one of Griffin's friends."

We said our goodbyes and left. We waited a moment until we were well away from Jenny's home before speaking.

"What did you think?" Griffin asked.

"She struck me as a kind, independent woman," I said. "Not a hint of unstable magic about her."

He nodded. "She's always been like that."

"Jenny didn't love Augustus, though, did she?" I asked.

"The best way to describe their relationship is one of tolerance. Jenny never has a bad word to say about Augustus, but unless prodded, she also never speaks about him. If I didn't know they were married, I'd think she lived alone."

"I thought the same thing when I looked around the house," I said. "It's like Augustus never lived there."

"Because he spent most of his time with his secret moor witch, misbehaving around his marriage vows," Hodgepodge said.

"I wondered if Jenny had fallen out of love with Augustus and used the stone heart amulet to destroy him, but having met her, I got nothing but kindness from her," I said.

"Using dark magic isn't her style," Griffin said. "And she had no clue where Augustus was."

"And no knowledge or interest in the statue. Can you check her alibi?" I asked.

"It'll be easy to do. I'll speak to the other ladies in the wreath-making group and pretend I want more details about their project. They'll be able to confirm if they were at Jenny's house on the night the statue was destroyed."

"Even before you've done that, I'm tempted to strike Jenny off the suspect list," I said.

"Which leads us back to who?" Griffin asked.

I wrinkled my nose. "It leads us back to the broken royal family who have no reservations about using magic. Whatever the cost."

Chapter 19

I finally got into the stone chamber at noon. The roof appeared intact and not as if two giant dragons had blasted through it last night. It was only when I peered closely that I saw the shimmer of magic holding an illusion in place. It was also much colder, revealing the air was whistling in through a magically concealed hole.

While I'd been away, more stone statues dotted the space the dragons had occupied. Shifting the statues around couldn't hide the lack of dragons, though, and visitors would soon ask where they'd gone.

Warwick strode in, barking orders at the guards who followed him. He spotted me, and after a few more minutes of conversation with his team, he dismissed them.

"How is everything?" he asked.

"Good. Griffin is looking after our new friends and, so far, no problems. How about the royal family?"

He looked around, ever alert. "Panicked and angry. They don't know what to do."

"We need them scared. And I need your help," I said.

"I'm already helping."

"And for that, I'm grateful, but I need to know where they all were the night Augustus's statue was destroyed. It has to be one of them. I've questioned Augustus's wife and his girlfriend. Although I haven't completely dismissed the girlfriend, every time I turn a corner in this mystery, it leads me back here."

Warwick mulled over my words. "It would have been easy for a member of the family to discover the stone heart amulet in the collection and realize its power. They seize the artifacts and forget about them, but if someone uncovered the truth, they could be testing the amulet."

"And now, it's got them around the throat, and they're out of control," I said. "Can you find out where each family member was the night of Augustus's death?"

"I don't need to find out. I already know. They were at the Feast of Gatland."

"Oh! Of course." Every year, there was a celebration on the anniversary of the Battle of Gatland. It marked the Ithric family's famous victory on the battlefield against a long-sworn enemy, the Fire Dagger Clan. "A family member could have left the feast and snuck to the stone chamber with the amulet."

"They'd have had an escort," Warwick said. "Lady Isolda would have insisted on it. She knows her family too well. They have a nasty habit of misbehaving if they aren't kept under her thumb."

"What about Lord Crosby? Or Grand Dame Ravenswood? Could they have gotten out of their turrets and be using the amulet?"

"Dame Ravenswood is an escape artist, but my guards have reported no recent breakouts. Lord Crosby stays content in his rooms. Lady Isolda ensures he takes strong sedatives, so even if he got out, he'd barely be able to move unaided. We can discount them."

"Double-check with your guards, just in case a member of the family is unaccounted for at any time."

"I'll see what I can do, but this is a dead end." Warwick continually scanned the room, always on the watch for trouble. "What about you?"

"I'm pretending it's business as usual," I said. "Then I'm off to visit our new friends in the forest."

"Take care, Bell. The family's rage will soon overspill, and they'll be looking for blood. I don't want you in the firing line."

"She won't be," Hodgepodge said. "I'll protect her."

"I'll be in touch." Warwick strode away, leaving me with a room full of people trapped in stone and a head full of questions.

"We keep reaching dead ends." I stood in front of Emberthorn and Stormwing. The stone chamber had closed early due to a lack of visitors as rumors spread the dragons were missing, so I'd come to the forest earlier than planned to update them on my progress.

"Keep searching," Emberthorn said, his scales brighter than last night. "You'll find the amulet soon. I have faith in you."

"Augustus's wife, Jenny, has an alibi for that night," I said. "Griffin confirmed she didn't have time to get to the castle when her friends left her home. Although she has a good motive for wanting him dead, she's content with her life. That comfort could be taken away once it's discovered Augustus won't be coming back. She'd lose too much by killing him."

"What about the witch girlfriend?" Stormwing was flopped on his belly, his eyes closed. His scales were still a dull red.

"She has a bad alibi but also cared little for Augustus. I got the impression she used him when she wanted a companion. Sabine shed no tears over his loss."

"You're taking too long to find out who the killer is," Stormwing said. "Brother, we shouldn't have employed an amateur."

"Bell's not under your employment," Hodgepodge snapped. "Or if she is, where is her payment?"

"Our emissary's payment is the privilege she feels from being around us," Stormwing said. "We should get paid to breathe in the stench of mortal."

"Forgive Stormwing," Emberthorn said. "Seraphina was here earlier and gave him a double dose of something unpleasant. He's had an upset stomach ever since."

"Keep my personal business out of your mouth," Stormwing said. "I don't trust Seraphina. She's poisoned me. My stomach feels as if I have a dozen rancid piglets dancing in it."

"It sounds like a bad case of trapped gas," I said. "Hodgepodge gets it when he's had a fatty meal or too much fruit."

"I do not! Well, I occasionally become bloated. It's nothing a belly rub doesn't cure," Hodgepodge said.

"Perhaps I could rub your belly," I said to Stormwing. "You could feel more comfortable."

Stormwing huffed out smoke then flopped onto his side, exposing a hugely distended stomach. "You have permission to touch me."

I bobbed a curtsy, hiding a smile, and got to work, using both hands and starting at the top of his stomach before massaging in vigorous circles.

"How goes things at the castle?" Emberthorn asked. "I've been getting updates from our new companions who have been taking care of us. Evander is a character."

"He's smug," Stormwing grumbled.

"I spoke to Warwick, and the royal family is stressed. They're pretending you've been taken for repair, but it won't be long before people learn the truth. Visitor numbers were way down today. Word is getting out that you're no longer in the chamber, and people don't want to see statues of people they don't know. It's hurting the family's fortunes."

"They'll be quick to react," Emberthorn said. "We must be prepared."

"No offense, but you and Stormwing aren't ready to fight. You were barely able to fly last night."

Emberthorn grumbled his disapproval. "I will admit, I was shocked by how much that short flight took out of me. We still have much healing to do, but no time to do it in."

"You take as much time as you need," I said. "We'll protect you."

"Has something died?" Hodgepodge gagged. "What is that disgusting smell?"

"That would be me," Stormwing said, not a hint of apology in his tone. "Bell's massage is most effective. The intestinal piglets are settling."

I tucked my scarf over my mouth and continued rubbing his belly. "I'm glad it's helping. It's what family does. We look after each other in good and bad times."

"Family!" Stormwing snorted. "I don't want a family of misfits and troublemakers. Oh, and liars."

I looked over my shoulder to discover Seraphina standing in the clearing. I stopped massaging Stormwing and hurried over to her. "Take a seat. You look like you're about to fall down."

She waved away my offer, remaining standing. "I'm just tired. I've already been to Leah for a tonic. It's my turn to look after the dragons again. And I have more healing potions to give them."

"You can barely look after yourself," Stormwing said. "Emissary, return and rub my stomach. The rancid piglets still need shifting."

"Ach! You ungrateful walloper." Hodgepodge jumped off my shoulder, scuttled over to Stormwing, and bit his foot.

Stormwing roared and attempted to stamp on Hodgepodge. "Disrespectful insect. I will crush you."

I grabbed Hodgepodge and held out a hand to Stormwing. "Behave! Or there'll be no more belly rubs."

"Is that what that smell is?" Seraphina joined me and grimaced. "I warned him there were side effects to the healing potions."

"I'm still convinced you're poisoning me." Stormwing thumped back onto his belly, and a large rasp came out of his rear end. "Aaaaa. That feels better."

"How is the healing going?" I asked Seraphina, my mouth and nose firmly buried in my scarf and my eyes watering.

Her face contorted as if she was chewing on something sharp. "It's good but slower than I'd like. I'm worried because I know the family is plotting to find the dragons."

"They can only cover their lies about where they've gone for so long," I said. "They want Emberthorn and Stormwing back, trapped in stone again."

She looked over at me, her expression weary. "Still no joy in finding Augustus's killer?"

"We've discounted a few suspects," I said. "And Warwick is double-checking the families' alibis. I forgot they held the Feast of Gatland on the night Augustus was destroyed. I'm wondering if one of them snuck out, though, and pushed over the statue."

"They're always under close guard," Seraphina said. "Lady Isolda trusts no one. She pretends she sends guards with them to protect them, but they act as her spies and report back on any rule breaks by her family."

"Do we trust Warwick to be honest?" Stormwing asked. "He's always been fiercely loyal to the royal family."

"You should trust me." Warwick stepped out of the shadows. "Because I'm here to report trouble is on its way. The family has summoned wraiths."

Chapter 20

"Wraiths! They wouldn't be so foolish." Seraphina lifted a shaking hand and settled it on her chest. "They were exiled because they couldn't be controlled. No amount of magic will contain them."

"I don't know how the family got them here, but I've seen them." Warwick strode closer, his expression grim. "I counted six. There could be more."

"What's a wraith?" I asked.

"Nothing good, by the sounds of it," Hodgepodge said.

Warwick formally greeted the dragons. "Wraiths are monsters of smoke and shadow, banished before my time and certainly yours. They're heartless beings whose focus is survival. To live, they must take others' lives."

"I definitely hate them now," Hodgepodge said. "We should have nothing to do with them."

Emberthorn growled. "Their interest is self-preservation, and they care nothing about who they hurt in order to survive."

"It doesn't sound like much of a life to me," Stormwing said. "We will destroy them."

Seraphina shook her head. "In your weakened condition, the wraiths are a danger to you too."

Stormwing snapped his teeth at her. "If it weren't for you, we wouldn't be in this position. It's all your fault they're here."

"Let's play the blame game another time." Warwick uncurled a long whip from his shoulder and handed it to me. "This is laced with an enchantment. It's one of the few things that will destroy wraiths without you having to get too close to them. And I'd advise you to stay as far away from them as you can. When they touch you, you're in trouble. And if they take enough of your life, you'll turn into a wraith and follow them."

I grabbed the whip's handle, and a surge of ancient power pulsed across my palm. "They can't know we're here, though. We're hidden. Magic is concealing us."

"The family has search parties heading out in all directions. It won't be long before someone talks about seeing the dragons flying this way. We must be prepared for whatever comes for them."

"We won't apologize for our indiscrete exit," Stormwing said. "We did our best to escape. Bell presented us with few options."

"We did what we had to do," I said. "It was go out through the roof or nothing."

Warwick nodded. "I must return to the castle before I'm missed. But I brought a new friend of yours to assist you."

Finn walked into the clearing. He nodded a greeting at all of us then extended a formal greeting to the dragons, bending low, and sweeping his wings wide.

"Showoff," Hodgepodge muttered. "I'm growing allergic to feathers."

Once the introductions had been made, Finn turned to me. "Warwick thought you may need a hand. I'm happy to look out for you. Whatever you need."

"I appreciate that. And we look out for each other," I said. "We won't be able to defeat these wraiths unless we work as a team."

"I must go. Be prepared for anything." Warwick's stern gaze slid around the group. He disappeared into the darkness as stealthily as he'd appeared.

Seraphina was still shaking. The dragons were silent, and Finn shifted from foot to foot, seeming uncertain what he should do to help.

"Let's get to work," I said. "We'll stay here because we have magic concealing us, but we'll set up a wide perimeter and watch for anything approaching."

"I can watch from up high," Finn said. "I'm happy to be in charge of air patrol."

"I have a bundle of trigger alerts," Seraphina said. "We have the magic wards, so no one should see us, but if the wraiths get through, the trigger will alert us to their presence."

She handed around small bundles of wrapped herbs that sparkled when touched. Finn took to the air to scout the area, while I worked with Hodgepodge and Seraphina to set a wide circular perimeter around the dragons.

"You should try that whip," Hodgepodge said.

"Try it on what?" I'd draped the whip clumsily over my shoulder.

"You need to get your whipping arm into shape. You don't want the first time you use it to be when a wraith is lurching toward you."

"They lurch?"

"Float. Chase. Bumble! I've never met one. But you must be ready."

I planted a trigger in the ground and lightly covered it with earth. I stood and uncoiled the whip. The ancient leather looked cracked, but it was slick with powerful magic. I tested it a few times, flicking it lightly across the ground.

"More effort," Hodgepodge said. "The enchantment will respond to your energy just as you respond to it."

I pulled back my shoulder and let the whip fly. A huge blast of light shot out and ricocheted against several trees, leaving dazzling sheens in my irises. "Wow! This is amazing."

Finn appeared above us and dropped to the ground. "Was that you?"

I nodded at him, smiling as I stared at the whip. "Warwick wasn't joking when he said this thing had power. I wonder where he got it."

"Most likely stolen from the family's private collection," Hodgepodge said. "They probably forgot they even owned it."

Finn's smile had a nervous edge to it. "I'm glad you've got it. I've never gone up against wraiths, but I've heard nothing good about them. They're banned from Crimson Cove. If they get too close, the wards kick them out. Be careful around them, though."

"I'll do whatever it takes to protect Emberthorn and Stormwing," I said. "We haven't come this far to lose them now."

Finn nodded as he paced around.

"Is something wrong?"

He turned to me, his expression unusually tense. "I wanted to warn you about my demon side. Stay away from me if I turn. I get ugly."

I studied him for a few seconds then moved on to plant the next trigger. "Is there anything I can do to stop your demon side from coming out?"

"He's unpredictable." Finn followed me, taking a handful of triggers so he could help plant them.

"I've got a solution for stopping your demon if he turns mean." Hodgepodge leapt off my shoulder. He shook himself from snout to tail, and a swirl of magic flew around him, transforming him into a stunning giant wyvern with shimmering scales. "I loathe being this big. I feel clumsy and uncoordinated. I don't know how the dragons manage. But if Finn's demon gets out of control, I'm happy to stamp on him. That'll slow him."

"You may need to stamp hard." Finn's expression remained serious. "My demon side is a giant jerk. He's a chaos demon, and he loves nothing more than to add fuel to a fiery situation. He'll see the wraiths coming after the dragons as a source of entertainment and will delight in making things more complicated."

"You won't do any of that if you're squashed under my foot." Hodgepodge swished his tail, knocking Finn over.

I hurried to help him up, but Finn was already getting to his feet. "I won't be offended if you come for me,

Hodgepodge. Whatever you have to do to keep Bell and the dragons safe."

"You can control yourself," I said. "I believe in you. But we must deal with these wraiths quickly, so I can focus on finding who is using the stone heart amulet. They're seriously out of control. They're a risk to all of us, and they're only getting worse."

"Are you worried about the dragons?" Finn asked.

We returned to planting the triggers on the ground.

"Emberthorn has confirmed the amulet will slow them, maybe even kill them in their weakened state, so, yes, I'm worried."

Finn planted the last trigger and brushed dirt off his hands.

"Shouldn't you be air patrolling?" Hodgepodge asked. "I don't like how close you're lingering to Bell. And is that demon sulfur I can smell? Do I need to stamp on you already?"

"I'm backing off." Finn chuckled. "I'll go look. But it was all clear when I was up there a few moments ago. The wraiths still don't know we're here." He zoomed into the air and hovered, turning in a slow circle.

"You don't have to be so mean," I whispered to Hodgepodge. "Finn is helping us when we're in dire straits. He didn't have to come here."

"I do! He's a tricky half-demon who has a crush on you."

"He's a friend! And he's a half-angel."

"You act like it's more than friendship. You blush whenever he shows up."

"I... Maybe I do. But now's not the time to think about that. We have wraiths to deal with, dragons to protect, and an out-of-control killer to stop. My plate is full enough."

"Good. You've seen sense. We don't need the added complication of a dubious angel in the mix."

I looked up at Finn. He was frozen in midair, then he dived and landed, one knee on the ground. "They're coming!"

I gripped the whip handle. "The wraiths? So soon?"

"Yes! We need to go back to the dragons." Finn grabbed my hand, and we ran together, Hodgepodge lumbering behind us, knocking into trees and flattening bushes.

"How many?" I asked.

"I saw a dozen."

"How do they know we're here?"

"Someone must have talked," Finn said. "No time to worry about that now. We need to be ready. Show no sympathy for these creatures. They have no souls. They live to destroy. That's their ambition in life. Chaos and misery."

We emerged into the clearing, and Emberthorn and Stormwing instantly got to their feet, sensing something was wrong.

"The wraiths are coming," I said.

"Which direction?" Seraphina asked.

Finn pointed toward the castle. "They were skimming above the trees. A line of them. A dozen wraiths."

"Coming straight for us," Emberthorn said, his large nostrils flaring. "I thought we would have more time."

"The time to hide is over. We must fight," Finn said.

The night was thick with shadows, and the air hummed with an eerie stillness as we stood together, a motley group of protectors, surrounded by the ancient trees. Finn, his wings drawn close, emanated an otherworldly light, his eyes keen on the shifting darkness. Seraphina whispered incantations under her breath, a protective barrier forming around us. Hodgepodge stood alert in front of us, his scales glistening in the moonlight, a huge, powerful barrier against the encroaching attackers.

Finn gripped my hand and nodded at me. "We've got this. You've defeated much worse than a few mindless wraiths."

I held the handle of the enchanted whip, its power tingling in my palm. The dragons huddled close to each other, smoke pluming from their mouths. But they were unable to fight. We were their only line of defense against the wraiths that slithered through the night, getting closer with every second that passed.

A magical trigger exploded, and light blazed through the trees.

"Get ready!" I yelled, dropping Finn's hand and gripping the whip so tight my knuckles ached.

An icy breeze swept through the forest, and the wraiths materialized from the shadows. Figures made of smoke and malice, they glided toward us with a haunting grace.

Finn flared his wings, light sparkling across them, Seraphina conjured orbs of protective magic, and Hodgepodge let out a low growl that made the ground shake.

"Here they come!" Finn's voice cut through the tense air.

The first wraith lunged, smoke tendrils reaching for us. I cracked the whip, and a burst of light exploded from it, disintegrating the wraith into nothingness. But there were more, emerging from the depths of the forest like a relentless tide.

"Finn, cover the left side! Seraphina, reinforce the magic barrier. Hodgepodge, stay close to the dragons. Don't let the wraiths touch them." My commands echoed in the night as I swung the whip with precision.

Finn soared into the air, white magic crackling off his wings and slamming into our attackers. Seraphina's magic danced around us, a shimmering shield against the wraiths. Hodgepodge lunged at any wraith that dared come too close, snapping his jaws with deadly accuracy and turning them into wisps of smoke.

The forest erupted into chaos as more wraiths swirled around us, their haunting whispers echoing through the trees. A chill crawled up my spine, but there was no room for fear.

"Finn, on your right!" I shouted, my whip cracking through the air.

"They're relentless," Seraphina panted, beads of sweat on her forehead as she redoubled her efforts to keep Emberthorn and Stormwing safe.

The battle raged, but we fought with purpose. Finn's wings blasting more wraiths, Seraphina's magic flaring bright, and Hodgepodge roaring, a force of nature against the encroaching darkness.

Emberthorn and Stormwing breathed out smoke, and although I should choke on it, the scent filled me with energy. I swung the whip at the center of a group of wraiths. Light exploded, engulfing them with a crackle of power. They screeched, a chorus of agony, as they disintegrated into the night.

Silence fell over the forest. The remaining wraiths dissipated like smoke, leaving only echoes of their disturbing presence. Finn landed beside me. Seraphina lowered her hands, and Hodgepodge let out a triumphant roar.

As I crouched, ready for the next wraiths, an icy grip wrapped around my waist and lifted me off my feet. I yelped, unable to use the whip. Tendrils of fear flooded my thoughts, and I almost dropped my weapon.

Hodgepodge's head whipped around when he heard me, and he charged. He opened his mouth wide, giant, serrated teeth approaching at speed. At the last second, he moved his head and grabbed the wraith.

I tumbled to the ground, rolled onto my feet, and let the whip fly. The wraith vanished in a swirl of smoke and screams.

The whip's energy poured over me, but there was something else. My own magic surged. A hot wave of power flooded through me and almost took me to my knees with its strength. This was new.

Four more wraiths appeared and skulked toward me. I shot out the whip, taking out two with a crisp flick. The others dodged my attack. Emberthorn blasted smoke around me, hiding me from them and giving me time to gather my strength.

"There are more coming!" Finn yelled. "I see at least twenty."

"Gather around us," Emberthorn called out. "Don't split up. We are stronger together."

I backed up with Hodgepodge until I bumped into Emberthorn and pressed my back against his scales. Finn stood in front of Stormwing with Seraphina.

I was breathing so hard, I felt dizzy. I wouldn't give up on the dragons, but when that wraith grabbed me, it had left a circle of ice cold around me, and I couldn't get warm.

The wraiths approached, spread out in a long line, and formed a semicircle.

"Do not be scared, Bell," Emberthorn said. "You are much stronger than them. Don't let them feed off your terror."

"She has a right to be a little afraid," Hodgepodge grumbled. "These things are gross."

"Get ready, everyone," I yelled. "Don't let them reach the dragons."

The wraiths surged as one. Before they could get too close, magic blasted them from behind, obliterating half a dozen in a single attack.

Astrid, Griffin, and Evander appeared from the trees, magic blazing around them. Griffin twirled a sword that glowed and sparked. The wraiths, caught off guard, hissed and turned toward the newcomers. Astrid unsheathed a gleaming blade, and Evander hurled orbs of magic with effortless precision.

"Let's give the wraiths a warm welcome!" Astrid's battle cry rang out. "Show them what we're made of."

The wraiths recoiled under the vicious attack. Griffin's magical sword crackled through the air, disrupting their shadowy forms. Astrid's blades flew free, a seemingly endless supply she flung with precision, severing smoke tendrils. Evander moved like a phantom among our enemy, striking with calculated ferocity.

The attack shattered the wraiths' cohesion. They scattered, their haunting whispers turning into desperate cries. Griffin's sword, Astrid's blades, and Evander's agility created a symphony of destruction they were powerless to stop.

"Back to the shadows where you belong," Griffin taunted, his eyes ablaze with determination, echoes of his former proud military experience making him appear taller and almost scary.

The wraiths, outnumbered and outmaneuvered, melted like a nightmare at dawn, and the forest fell silent.

"That was fun." Evander sauntered over. "You should have said you were inviting soul-draining shadow nightmares. We'd have arrived sooner."

Astrid wiped a streak of wraith essence from her blade. "Bell, you good?"

I nodded. As the adrenaline of the skirmish faded, I felt a surge of gratitude for my friends. We'd defeated an enemy, and the dragons were safe.

But for how long?

Chapter 21

We spent twenty minutes checking and patrolling, but no more wraiths appeared. We reset the magic triggers so we'd get an alert if anything came close then gathered with the dragons. Astrid, Griffin, and Evander formally greeted them.

"You are all welcome, Bell's assistants," Emberthorn said.

"We're Bell's assistants?" Evander cocked an eyebrow. "I see myself as more of a rescuer of damsels in distress. The heroic warrior who rides into battle, fearless—"

"And full of his own sense of self-importance and hot air," Griffin said. "We're happy to be Bell's assistants. Her actions inspire us to do more. She was the one who always believed you would come back."

"We're a team," I said. "We're equals."

"You're an emissary," Stormwing said. "That sets you apart from everybody."

I shook my head, not liking that idea. "An emissary is only as effective as the people she surrounds herself with. I'd be nothing without my friends. Friends, I consider more like my family, no matter if you consider us untrustworthy misfits, Stormwing."

He had the decency to duck his head. "I spoke out of turn because of my guts."

"What's this?" Evander's eyes gleamed with amusement.

"Dragon gas. Be happy you missed it," I murmured.

Hodgepodge shook himself, returning to his normal size. He leapt on my shoulder and snuggled close to my face.

"Good work, Hodgie." I kissed his head.

"I still think little of being giant, but it comes in useful when danger gets too close or gassy dragons want to stamp around and make a nuisance of themselves." He glared at Stormwing.

"We should celebrate our victory," Evander said.

"Don't speak too soon." Astrid turned away from the group, her shoulders tense and a blade in her hand. "Something feels wrong."

"More wraiths?" I joined her and peered through the trees, my heart kicking up a gear. A dense fog was approaching at speed, full of magic sparks. "What in the name of all things unholy dragon is that?"

A flash of magic shot toward me, and Hodgepodge leapt off my shoulder into the path of the spell. The magic blasted into his chest, and he flipped in the air before turning to stone.

I grabbed him before he hit the ground and shattered. I fell to my knees, cradling him against my chest. "Hodgie! No!"

A cold, crazed laughter slid out of the dense fog, rattling through my bones as its familiarity whacked into me.

Finn was instantly by my side, his hand on my arm. "Bell, move! You're vulnerable. Whoever is in that fog has the stone heart amulet."

Tears clogged my throat as I scrambled to my feet. "He got Hodgepodge. He saved me."

Finn tugged me back into the protective circle of the dragons and my friends, my feet not wanting to move and my head unable to process what had just happened to my best friend.

"I recognize that nasty laugh," Evander muttered. "But it can't be him. He's dead."

"So do I. It's Prince Godric." I clutched Hodgepodge to me. "Seraphina, can you do anything for Hodgepodge?"

She blinked at me with wide eyes. "I'll look at him, but I'm promising nothing. Stone magic is beyond me."

I carefully passed her Hodgepodge, reluctant to release him from my protective embrace. "Whatever you do, don't break him or I'll never get him back."

More laughter rumbled out of the fog, but there was still no sign of Prince Godric. He was taunting us.

A sizzle of magic knocked Finn off his feet, and he rolled several times before landing on his face in front of Emberthorn's claws. More magic blasted out of the fog, and the air was tinged with heat and ash.

An invisible force squeezed my throat and yanked me off my feet, dragging me toward the trees. As I struggled, a ring of stone surrounded my friends and the dragons, separating us. I could hear their yells as the stone encased them, forming a dome over their heads and trapping them. The stone shuddered and remained intact, and I could imagine Emberthorn and Stormwing kicking it to get free.

"All alone again, little cleaner?" Prince Godric's deranged voice slid through the fog. "Why is it that people always abandon you? Not worth loving, I suppose."

I rubbed the ring of strength on my finger. It may be of no use in a battle against wraiths, but it would be effective in defeating a prince. "Show yourself, coward."

"You don't tell me what to do. If you want me, you find me. And then you grovel on your knees and hope I'll spare your friends' lives. Yours, however, is over."

The tightness around my neck vanished, and through the fog, I saw a flash of movement and chased it. That had to be the twisted prince, and I was taking him down.

"You'll have to try harder than that," Prince Godric mocked. "Hurry! Or more of your pathetic friends will die."

"You're supposed to be dead," I yelled. "How did you survive?"

"I could be a delusion," he said. "You're clearly insane if you think you can save the dragons."

I turned, trying to find his location through the fog. "I have saved them. They're free from your prison."

"They'll soon be back where they belong. That's if I don't decide to roast them and scatter their ashes to the four corners of the world."

"They're exactly where they need to be. Back in the realm they deserve to rule without your family's interference."

"Traitor! You should be loyal to my family."

"You don't inspire loyalty. You inspire fear. The people are done with you. They want your family off the throne and the dragons back." I turned in a circle, desperate to find Prince Godric and get my revenge. "That's what I'll make happen."

"With your mop and bucket?" He cackled a laugh. "I'll take great pleasure in destroying you. Although I'll keep you alive long enough to watch me decimate those weak excuses for dragons. They will never rule. They can barely stand."

"If you're not afraid of them, why encase them in stone? And why kill Augustus? You have the amulet, so it must have been you." Now I knew Prince Godric had the stone heart amulet, I was in no doubt he was behind all of our troubles.

"Him! That worm barely deserved my notice, yet he spoke out against me. He deserved what he got. And once I had a taste of what this magic could do, I refused to stop. Anyone who wronged me, looked at me strangely, or I didn't like, felt my revenge. And they will continue to feel it until all my enemies are destroyed."

"You knocked over the statue because you didn't like Augustus? What's wrong with you?"

"I'm a prince! Everyone must obey me. Augustus couldn't keep his wicked tongue quiet, so I taught him a lesson."

I skirted around a giant oak tree. "Show yourself if you're so determined everyone must face your cruel discipline."

There was silence. My heartbeat rang in my ears, my gaze never settling as I hunted for the broken prince. From his tone, I sensed his madness. The stone heart amulet had twisted him into something unnatural. A thing that must be stopped.

"It would be my pleasure," Prince Godric snarled. "Let me start by introducing you to a real dragon."

The ground shook, and I tensed, the whip in one hand and the ring of power sparking on my finger. The fog turned into hot smoke, and embers danced in the air as an enormous, bulky shape appeared.

My mouth dropped open as a yellow dragon with a huge metal harness and a cage around its head loomed into view. Prince Godric sat on its back.

He screeched a laugh when he saw my shock. "You're not the only one who can control the dragons."

I blinked away my horror. "You're not controlling that creature. You're torturing it. Release it from that cage. It must be in agony."

The dragon roared and stamped its front feet.

"You're just like my family. They always underestimated me, too," Prince Godric said.

I could see him more clearly now the fog was less dense. His eyes were completely black, and his skin was corpse-gray and bloated. Around his neck was a glowing amulet. The stone heart amulet. That must be keeping him alive. However Prince Godric had done it, he'd resurrected himself from a watery grave. But what had come back was entirely unnatural, and my stomach churned at his twisted, broken form. And the smell! Like overripe eels left in the sun.

"Stunned you into silence, have I?" He leered at me. "I'm getting back what I'm entitled to. This is my first step to getting everything I deserve. Kill her!"

I dodged out of the way as the dragon shot a ragged jet of flames at me. One glimpse into its eyes showed it was close to madness. Whatever Prince Godric had done to this poor creature had tipped its mind over the edge.

"You can't run forever," Prince Godric yelled over the wall of flames. "We'll catch you, eventually. When I return you to my family and reveal you as a traitor, you'll wish you'd never been born. I'll convince my mother to destroy the dragons, and in return, she'll pry herself off the throne and give me the power I should have had all this time."

"If you ever gain control, this realm will be ruined." I was hidden behind a tree, figuring out my next move. I longed for Hodgepodge to be wrapped around my neck, but he remained powerless while confined in a prison of stone. Seraphina would free him. She had to.

I focused on my dangerous situation. I had to get to Prince Godric and remove the amulet. Without it, I wouldn't be able to reverse the power that had Hodgepodge trapped.

"Come out, little cleaner. Once you're captured, I'll deal with your irritating friends. Was that Seraphina I saw as a betrayer, too? She was always obsessed with those beasts. I told Mother not to trust her, but she insisted on keeping her around. Now I can prove I was right all along."

I ducked and shuffled to the next tree. If I could get behind the dragon, I could scale it by running up its tail, grab Prince Godric, and yank the amulet off his neck. Once I had it, he'd have to stop fighting. Maybe without its protective magic, he'd die.

"If you don't come out, I'll bring the stone prison down on your friends' heads. Even if they managed to survive, they'd be grievously injured and vulnerable to my pet's attack. Perhaps I could add them to my statue collection. Do you like my pretty creations?"

I didn't speak. Prince Godric was goading me, attempting to draw me out so he could attack again with his deranged dragon.

"It will be your fault if they die." His voice was full of hatred and frustration. "Give yourself to me, and they will live. Admittedly, it'll be a short life in my dungeon, but you could spare them. It's the right thing to do, and you're one of those sickeningly good people who always do the right thing. Don't stop now."

I stood behind the dragon, and sadness overwhelmed my heart as I saw its flanks covered in cuts and bruises. Prince Godric must have beaten this creature into submission. The rank tang of twisted magic that flowed around it proved to me this dragon didn't want to attack me. Prince Godric had harnessed its power and was misusing it.

I dodged out from behind the tree and raced toward the dragon's tail. I leapt onto it and scrambled up its back. It roared, flicking its head back and swishing its tail from side to side. But I kept scrambling, getting closer to Prince Godric. I lunged and wrapped my arm around his throat.

He yelped out his surprise and grabbed me, dirty fingernails digging into my flesh. We were sent flying by the rearing dragon. I refused to let go and laced my fingers around the amulet's chain. We hit the ground with a bone-jarring thud and rolled several times.

The dragon stomped and snarled, one foot slamming an inch from my head.

I was on my back, Prince Godric on top of me, facing the sky so I could smell his unwashed hair. I yanked on the amulet's chain, but the metal dug into my fingers, and it refused to break.

"You will not have my amulet, you worthless, annoying drudge! Everywhere I turn, there you are. It's time you knew your place," he roared.

"And it's time you knew yours. You have no right to rule." I tugged the chain again. "You're cold, heartless, and cruel. How can you expect the realm to thrive under such savage conditions?"

"I will thrive! I'll get everything I desire. I deserve it. Let go of me, you common piece of dirt." Prince Godric writhed on top of me, attempting to slam his head into my nose. I dodged the blow by turning my head. I couldn't let him go. If he got loose, he wouldn't hesitate to use the stone heart amulet on me and then smash me to pieces.

The dragon's tail slammed into Prince Godric, and I lost my grip on him as he flew through the air and smashed into a tree. I scrambled to my feet and ran. I shot out the whip, and Prince Godric yelped as it made contact. But he wouldn't go down. No matter what I did, this broken prince wasn't giving up.

He turned and snarled at me, no trace of humanity on his face. "You have breathed your last breath." His hand went to the stone heart amulet, and it glowed under his touch.

I had to find a place to hide. A place the stone magic couldn't touch me. If I was stopped, Hodgepodge would be trapped forever. I would not lose my best friend. I had to defeat Prince Godric.

The air filled with heat and dragon roars. Emberthorn slammed to the ground beside me, Evander and Griffin on his back, magic swirling around them. Stormwing was close behind, Astrid riding him. He clumsily descended next to his brother, and Astrid slid off, blades in her hands.

"Stay back! Nobody move or I'll destroy you. Anyone who comes at me, I will turn into stone." Prince Godric held out the amulet, his black eyes liquid pools of fetid hatred. "It's your choice. Anyone who wants to be a hero, step forward, or stay your illegal magic and live to breathe for another day."

Nobody moved. We watched Prince Godric's descent into madness as he cackled and stamped around, lobbing out threats and roaring his anger as the amulet pulsed and sparked.

My whip couldn't defeat him, and I wasn't fast enough to reach him and pummel him using the ring of strength. I needed something else. I fumbled in the pockets of my underskirt, my hand closing around my small compact mirror. "Hey! Godric."

"Bell! Don't taunt the insane prince with the powerful amulet," Evander said. "You saw what he did to Hodgepodge."

"I'm getting justice. Godric, stop picking on people," I yelled.

"I am your prince! And you will address me as such."

I shook my head as I walked toward him, the compact mirror in my grasp. "You're nothing but a child in a man's body. You respect no one, including yourself. You're a disgrace to your family. It's no wonder your mother has overlooked you so many times. Did you know she mocks you behind your back? You're an embarrassment to her. She doesn't miss you. No one does."

"I will have your head for those words!" Prince Godric held out the amulet, and a blast of magic shot toward me. I lifted the mirror, and the magic slammed into it and ricocheted back. Prince Godric didn't even have the time to gasp as the stone magic engulfed him.

There was a second of silence, and then Evander whooped a cheer and scooped me into his arms.

I gripped his shoulders as he twirled me. "Emberthorn, Stormwing. There's a dragon who needs your help."

"We've already seen her," Emberthorn said. "That was very brave, Bell."

"Some may say foolish." Stormwing waddled to the downed yellow dragon who had slumped to the ground the second Prince Godric had fallen off her back.

"It was downright insane." Astrid joined us and hugged me. "What if that spell hadn't hit the mirror? Or the mirror shattered?"

"It was the only way to defeat Prince Godric." I looked around. "Where are Seraphina and Finn?"

Astrid's smile faded. "They stayed with Hodgepodge. They're working on a plan to get him back."

"They can fix him?" Hope lifted my shredded heart.

"I'm... I'm not sure. They were talking about magic and the amulet," Griffin said.

"Have hope, Bell. We did it!" Evander said. "We stopped the wraiths, protected the dragons, and you took down Prince Godric. I call that a win."

I nodded as I walked over to Prince Godric, my knees not steady, and my heart not full of the hope Evander talked about. The amulet around Prince Godric's neck had also turned into stone. It was useless.

Was that the only way I could bring back Hodgepodge? Had I destroyed the one thing that would bring back my best friend and all the people Prince Godric had trapped?

Chapter 22

I cradled Hodgepodge as I walked. In his stone form, Hodgepodge was almost too heavy to carry, but I wasn't letting him go. I'd never let him go, no matter how many sad looks my friends exchanged.

As soon as we were out of danger, I'd raced back to find Hodgepodge. The others had stayed to deal with the injured yellow dragon, but I was walking back toward them with Seraphina and Finn on either side of me.

I glanced at Seraphina. "Is there another stone heart amulet?"

She shook her head. "There was only one made. When its creator realized how dangerous it was and how the magic hooked into the user and bespelled them, she made no more."

"Whoever created the amulet can do it again, though," I said. "We need to find her."

"She is long gone," Seraphina said. "That amulet was forged over a thousand years ago."

I swallowed down the lump in my throat. "You know people! Other powerful magic users."

Finn rested a hand on my shoulder. He said nothing, but that didn't stop the tears from making me want to choke. We'd stopped Prince Godric, but the cost was too high. I wouldn't lose Hodgepodge.

We found Astrid, Evander, and Griffin had bound the yellow dragon in powerful magic constraints. Emberthorn and Stormwing looked on, clearly exhausted, as they struggled to remain on their feet. The escape from the stone prison and the short flight through the forest had taken it out of them and would set back their recovery.

"How's he doing?" I asked Emberthorn, my gaze on the quiet, restrained dragon.

"*She* will require extensive rehabilitation. Prince Godric used deeply unpleasant magic on her to subdue her." His eyes glistened with concern.

"You removed the cage from her head. You're not worried she'll attack?"

Emberthorn's gaze went to Hodgepodge. "She is more comfortable without it and is too broken to fight back."

"Speak for yourself. She almost bit my arm clean off." Evander's right sleeve was shredded, and there was fresh blood on his skin.

"The dragon will heal, though?" I asked.

Emberthorn looked at Seraphina, and she nodded.

"Where did she come from?" I asked.

"Unfortunately, there are twisted individuals who capture weak dragons. This one recently gave birth, and producing a dragon egg is an exhausting process," Emberthorn said. "Someone must have captured her while she was recovering."

"Where's her baby? Not taken, too?"

"Most likely taken as leverage to ensure she behaved," Stormwing grumbled and stamped his feet. "And if we catch the person who took her egg, I will roast them until there's nothing left but ash."

Finn raised his eyebrows. "A lost dragon egg, you say. That must be a rare occurrence."

"It's almost unheard of," Emberthorn said.

"When we have a moment, I need to talk to you. I might be able to help with that."

"Do you know who took her egg?" Emberthorn growled low in his chest and stomped a foot close to Finn. "That's a serious crime. The mother would have been devastated. She wouldn't have been in her right mind. It would be the only way Prince Godric could have captured her."

"She's in the right place now," I said, a soothing note in my voice. "We'll look after her. Get her strong again. Won't we, Seraphina?"

She nodded again. "Healing three dragons won't be any more difficult than helping two. The potions I use will be the same. I'll just need to make more."

"You've hardly been helping us," Stormwing said. "My stomach still isn't right. And my head aches. I should be able to fly effortlessly by now."

"Hush, brother. We're all doing the best we can." Emberthorn's gaze returned to Hodgepodge. "Bell, I am sorry for your loss. Hodgepodge was a brave, loyal wyvern."

The tears threatened again as I clutched the cold stone form of my best friend. "He is so much more than that. He's family. I'm not giving up. I'm getting him back."

Stormwing looked at Prince Godric's stone statue. "How? The stone heart amulet has been destroyed."

My fingers curled around Hodgepodge. I'd had no option but to act. Prince Godric had been insane enough to turn us all to stone, and he'd cared nothing for who he hurt in his quest to get the power he desired.

"You did the right thing, Bell," Emberthorn said.

I shook my head. "It was stupid."

"You saved us." Astrid walked over and rested a hand on Hodgepodge's head. "If it weren't for your quick thinking, Prince Godric would be riding off on his captured dragon, taking Emberthorn and Stormwing to the castle. Everything you worked so hard to achieve would be undone."

A part of me didn't care. I just wanted Hodgepodge. I wanted to be snuggled in our cozy chair, reading a book, and dozing under a warm blanket next to the open fire. I wanted to tease Hodgepodge for eating too many cookies and then needing his belly rubbed. I wanted everything back the way it was.

I looked at Emberthorn, Stormwing, and the new dragon. My heart may feel shattered, but my grief wasn't as big as the situation I found myself in. Once we got the dragons back as our rulers, the realm would recover. But that wouldn't give me back my heart. My Hodgepodge.

"I wouldn't advise staying here much longer," Evander said. "I think we got all the wraiths, but one could have slipped away. If it returned to the castle, the royal family will know something was going on out here. They'll send more trouble our way."

"We can move Emberthorn and Stormwing," Seraphina said. "We have the backup site. It's a long walk or a short flight, whatever you feel up to doing."

"Long walk," Stormwing said. "Juniper can't fly."

"Juniper?" I looked at the yellow dragon who was laid flat out, her legs splayed, and her breathing rapid.

"We'll move her with magic," Astrid said. "I have a few spells up my sleeve, and no doubt, pretty boy here has the same. It'll take effort, but we can do it."

Evander was inspecting his damaged arm, but he nodded.

"I have something that will help, too." Seraphina was already looking through her backpack. "We'll get the dragons safely tucked away."

I was too tired and heartbroken to ask for more details. I hadn't given up on Emberthorn or Stormwing, but I had a more immediate problem to focus on. Everyone got to work, although Finn remained by my side.

"You should help them," I said. "Moving three exhausted, testy dragons is no easy task."

"I'm staying here. You need me."

"You can't help. Nobody can." My words were bitter-tinged as I gently stroked Hodgepodge.

Finn gripped my elbow to capture my attention. "Bell, do you trust me?"

I wasn't looking at him as I spoke. "I don't know you."

"You do! I looked after Hodgepodge at my sanctuary and healed him. And you trusted me enough to help me when my boss was almost poisoned. You didn't have to help me and my friends in Crimson Cove, but you did."

"Because I'm a softhearted idiot," I said. "Look where it's gotten me."

"It's gotten you everywhere! You've helped so many people, and this is just the beginning."

"What about Hodgepodge? Why should I have to make this sacrifice and lose him? How is that fair? Everyone tells me I have a good heart and see the best in everyone. That naivety means Hodgepodge is dead. He always complained about me being too trusting. He was right all along."

Finn was silent for a few seconds. "Hodgepodge isn't dead. Just trapped."

"The one thing that could release him, I destroyed," I said. "I put the needs of everyone else before my own. Hodgepodge has always been there for me. He's never left my side, no matter what happened. And I repaid him by doing this." My tears fell freely, and I let them drop onto the ground and hit Hodgepodge, staining his stone a darker grey.

Finn gave me a moment to cry before gently lifting my chin with a finger. "Because of your goodness. Bell, you're surrounded by allies. Everyone wants to help make this right."

I gulped back a sob. "The one thing they can't help me with is the one thing I want the most. I need Hodgepodge back. I can't go on without him. If I have to see his stone statue every day, it'll destroy me."

"Then let me help," Finn said. "To do that, you have to trust me."

"What can you do? Make another stone heart amulet? Seraphina already said the magic user who created the original one has been dead for a long time."

"That kind of magic is beyond me, but my demon flame burns hot and powerful."

"What good is that to me?"

He hesitated. "I may be able to crack open Prince Godric's statue and extract the amulet. Or destroy it. By destroying it, its power will release, and all those who have been turned to stone will be free."

I stared up at him, my breathing ragged as a tiny burst of hope spun around my heart. "You know for sure that's what will happen?"

"It's a working theory. With the amulet destroyed, its power will be neutralized." Finn held up a hand. "I feel it in my gut that this will work."

"I definitely don't know your gut enough to trust that theory."

"My gut is an excellent detector of right and wrong." He smiled. "I get a sense about people as soon as I meet them. It happened when I met Juno and Zandra. Did you know, when we first met, they were murder suspects?"

I furrowed my brow. "Maybe. But you thought they were innocent?"

"I knew they were. My partner didn't. He wanted to arrest them and charge them with murder, but I knew they were good people."

"Because... your gut told you?"

"It tells me a lot of things. Often that I'm hungry, but also when I'm right about something." Finn caught hold of my shoulders. "I can do this. Let me get Hodgepodge back for you."

I licked my lips, tasting the salt of my tears. "Will blasting Prince Godric's statue with your demon fire free him, too?"

Finn grimaced. "That would be an unfortunate side effect. All the statues in the castle will be free, so will Hodgepodge, but your delightful prince will also be back. And when he's released, he will come for you. You need to be ready for that."

I drew in a shaky breath and looked at Hodgepodge. "What if you get it wrong?"

"It's a calculated risk. And there's something else you need to be aware of."

I leaned over Hodgepodge and kissed his stone head. I looked up at Finn. "There are more complications?"

Finn nodded, his intense gaze grave. "When I turn full demon, I'll need controlling. Can you do that?"

I gulped, a mixture of fear and uncertainty spiraling in my gut like a poorly baked meat pie. "I'll do anything to bring Hodgepodge back."

"I'm not a friendly demon," Finn said. "And we should stay away from everyone else, in case this goes wrong. If my demon sees Emberthorn and Stormwing so weak, he'll have endless amounts of fun before destroying them."

"I don't want the others involved," I said. "If anyone is getting hurt, it'll be me. You're only doing this because I want Hodgepodge back."

"I want to see you smile again. I hate seeing your eyes filled with tears and your heart hurting. And I like Hodgepodge. He has a sharp tongue, but he looks out for you. You need a companion like that."

"Give me a minute. I'll arrange things with the others." I hurried away, my heart beating fast. There was a chance to get Hodgepodge back, and I was grabbing it, even if I had to face down Finn's demon to achieve success.

Once I'd checked in with Seraphina and let her know she was in charge of getting the dragons to our backup haven, I dashed back to Finn. "Let's move. The sooner we do this, the better."

Finn grabbed the statue of Prince Godric and heaved him along with us. "I want to keep this jerk in my line of sight. The first sign he's coming back to life, I'm taking him out."

We found a quiet place in the woods, surrounded by a bank of high, spiky-leaved bushes so we wouldn't be seen. Finn set Prince Godric's statue down and encouraged me to place Hodgepodge on the ground, too.

"My flame will scorch through anything, so you don't want to stand too close," Finn said.

"You said pain controls your demon," I said. "What level of pain are we talking?"

Finn pointed at the whip that was slung over my shoulder and the ring on my finger. "Use them. Don't hold back. Pain helps me keep a grip on my good side. I'll be battling with the demon from the inside, and I need you fighting for me out here. It won't be pretty. I'll be cruel to you. I'll want to hurt you."

"I know the cruelty won't be coming from the real you," I said.

"This demon may be a part of me, but he's a part I rejected a long time ago." Finn took a deep breath and swooped his wings. "Are you ready to meet him?"

Chapter 23

My breath stuttered and my pulse pounded as Finn's glorious white wings glittered with red sparks of demon energy before transforming into dense, dull black feathers, the tips ragged and burned. Although Finn's face changed little, his eyes glowed red, and the normally easy-going smile on his face transformed into a snarl as curls of smoke drifted off his body.

He cocked his head, and his gaze roved over me. "I've been watching you. You've captured our attention. Attractive, commonsense, uncomplicated."

"I know you, too." I held the whip in one hand, partly crouched in readiness to strike.

"You think you do. Just as my angel side thinks he understands me. He thinks he controls me. In truth, he doesn't know the first thing about me. Perhaps a few decades trapped and unable to shine his irritating goodness over things will change his mind."

"This is a short vacation for you," I said. "If you've been watching, then you know what we need to do."

His top lip curled up, and flames flickered from his mouth. "I know what you'd like me to do. But what we want and what we get are usually different."

I didn't have time to play with the demon version of Finn. I flicked the whip at him and caught him on the cheek.

Finn raised his hand, pressing his fingers against the cut, then inspected the blood. He licked it off. He lunged at me, and I met his cheekbone with my fist, the power from the ring sending him flying. It slowed him for seconds before he raced toward me, ragged, smoking wings outstretched.

I brandished the enchanted whip, its tendrils crackling with energy. The ring of strength glowed, empowering my every move. We circled each other, the air thick with tension. A bitter wind swirled through the trees, carrying the scent of danger.

Finn attacked, his clawed hands slashing through the air. I dodged, the whip snapping out in retaliation. The enchanted strands danced with a life of their own, aiming for his demonic form. He twisted away, but the crack of the whip echoed through the forest as it grazed his side.

He snarled, eyes glinting with demonic glee.

I gritted my teeth. The forest blurred as we exchanged rapid blows, the whip leaving streaks of light in its wake. Finn's laughter grated on my nerves, a maddening soundtrack to our deadly dance.

I swung the whip in a wide arc, aiming for his wings. The tendrils wrapped around one wing, sizzling as they made contact. Finn roared, the demonic façade momentarily faltering. Seizing the opportunity, I yanked the whip, sending him crashing into a tree.

The ring of strength pulsed with power as I closed in. Finn staggered to his feet, his eyes a mix of rage and surprise at my effective attack. I lashed out with the whip, the strands entwining around him. With a swift tug, I pulled him toward me.

"Goodness beats evil every time," I hissed, my voice cutting through the tension.

The ring glowed brighter as it unleashed a surge of magic. The whip tightened its grip on Finn, constraining him. He writhed and snarled, tearing the whip from his damaged wing. He blasted out flame and shards of glowing rock, causing me to cringe from the heat.

A sharp shard sliced my thigh, and I cried out and hit the dirt, losing my grip on the whip.

Finn shook out his wings. He tipped back his head, and a jet of black and red fire blasted into the sky.

My lungs burning and the wound on my thigh making me want to scream, I rolled behind Prince Godric's statue. Finn's demon flame followed me and scored the statue from its base to its stone hairline. I screamed as the flames blasted around me, and a sickening crack tore through the air.

Stone shattered and slammed onto my head in small hard pieces. The heat was almost too much to bear, and I curled into a ball, protecting my head from more debris as fire rolled around me. The heat lessened as a final, deafening crack lashed through the air. Prince Godric's statue had been destroyed, along with the stone heart amulet.

I grabbed Hodgepodge and held him against my chest. He was pulsing. He was about to be destroyed, too. He wasn't getting free. "No! I will not lose you. Stay with me! Hodgepodge, do not leave me."

I stared up at demon Finn, my eyes burning with terror. He snarled, a guttural sound that sent shivers down my spine, and he took in a deep, ominous breath. His black wings flared out, casting a shadow that seemed to engulf everything. Smoke billowed from him like a sinister cloak.

Frantically, I fumbled for the whip, my fingers searching desperately in the chaos. But it wasn't there. Panic gripped me as Finn stepped closer. I was pinned and defenseless, my options evaporating like mist in the wind.

I kept Hodgepodge close, my heart pounding in my chest. I'd protect him at any cost, my determination a shield against the encroaching dread.

His stone form burned against my chest, pulsing ominously, the rhythm echoing the seconds ticking away. Finn's attack was imminent, a cruel countdown to my worst nightmare.

Rather than Hodgepodge's stone shattering, it cracked slowly, and his head appeared. He was alive!

Hodgepodge grumbled a curse word, shook himself, and the rest of the stone disintegrated.

I gaped at him, joy mingling with disbelief.

"I'm happy to see you too, lassie. Now, move aside. There's work to be done." Hodgepodge kissed my nose, leapt out of my arms, and super-sized. He blocked a blast of demon flame with his own fire, roaring intense flame at Finn.

My giant, perfect, beautiful, powerful wyvern surprised Finn so much that he was almost engulfed in the fire, but he batted it aside at the last second with his wings. He leaped away, leaving a trail of toxic smog and choking dust.

But Hodgepodge was faster, and he didn't hesitate. He lunged at Finn and grabbed him with his enormous teeth, lifting him and shaking him hard, then he tossed him against a tree.

I raced toward Finn, who lay in a crumpled heap. "Are you... okay?" Dumb question, but I was still processing that my glorious Hodgepodge was back.

Finn laughed and held up a hand. "You'll have to kill me to get rid of me. Angel Finn is gone for good. This realm reeks of cruelty and hardship. I thrive in these conditions. He made a mistake by letting me loose in this broken place."

"I'll force you out," Hodgepodge said. "Bell, stand aside and let me stamp him."

I shook my head as I stood over Finn. "I know you're still in there. You love life. You love helping people. You will come back to me."

"He's gone." Demon Finn cackled a laugh, the sound full of bubbles. "You got what you wanted. The stone heart amulet is destroyed, and everyone is free. Consider Angel Finn's sacrifice a worthy one. I have this body now, and I intend to keep it."

I crouched. There was no need to restrain Finn since he'd been so badly weakened from Hodgepodge's attack. "You said you needed pain to come back, but I disagree."

"Give me pain! I love it."

"You'll love this more." I grabbed his shoulders and kissed him.

For a second, Finn struggled, but I held on tight and kept my lips pressed firmly against his, the taste of grit and dust in my mouth. Goodness beat evil every time, and I believed my good heart would defeat this demon's cruelty.

Finn stopped fighting. The redness in his eyes faded, and his wings returned to white.

I pulled back from our kiss and looked at the wonderfully familiar face of my new angelic friend. I smiled at him. "Thank you. You saved Hodgepodge."

Finn stared at me with wide blue eyes. "Right back at you. Bell, you saved my life. You defeated my demon."

It was late, just past midnight, and I'd been pretending not to be exhausted all day. Our adventures in the forest the previous evening felt like they'd happened over twenty-four hours ago. The dragons had been taken to a new haven and were recuperating under Seraphina's careful watch. My friends had snuck back to their normal lives and weren't acting as if they'd fought an insane prince who we'd thought was dead and rescued another dragon under the thrall of toxic magic.

And Hodgepodge and me? We'd returned to our lodgings with a very tired, confused half-angel, half-demon with us. Finn had collapsed in the chair in the corner of the room and fallen into a deep sleep.

I'd slept too but had needed to act as if nothing unusual had happened, so I'd gone to the castle to begin a normal day of work. What greeted me was a huge mess in the stone chamber, and all the statues were gone. The destruction of the stone heart amulet freed everyone. And all that was left for me to do, and it was no small task, was to clear the shattered remains and field dozens of curious questions from castle staff and visitors.

Of course, I knew nothing. I was only the cleaner. I showed up, took my orders, and got to work.

"We should postpone tonight's gathering." Hodgepodge was almost asleep, wrapped around my neck. He'd been there all day and had barely moved, other than when Lady Isolda briefly visited the stone chamber, muttering her disapproval about the vandalism and what was becoming of this world.

I was glad to have him with me. My heart was healed, and I couldn't be happier to have Hodgepodge coiled around me, exactly where he belonged. And it was all thanks to Finn.

"It's too late to postpone. Besides, I want to see everyone," I murmured. "They've all been busy keeping watch over the dragons, and I want to know about our new addition to the family. We have a new dragon, and she is beautiful."

"We'll do it tomorrow night. It feels like weeks since we've snuggled in our chair under a blanket with a plate full of cookies and a good book."

"We'll do that soon, I promise." Before I'd opened my front door, Evander appeared on the other side, grinning at me. "I thought that was you. Get in here. We've been waiting."

I dragged my feet as I shuffled inside, cheered by the sight of my friends. Finn was still in the easy chair, though he was awake. He gave me a tired smile. Griffin, Astrid, Seraphina, and Warwick were also there.

"I told you idiots we should have done this another night." Astrid strode over and peered into my face. "You're dead on your feet. I bet those psychos in the castle didn't let you use magic to clear up the remains, did they?"

"I used a little when no one was around," I said. "But it was a lot of backbreaking work."

"I can't believe Lady Isolda made you do that all on your own," Astrid tutted. "Monster."

"She said it was my job. Although, I'm not sure I'll have a job for much longer. The dragons are gone, and all the stone statues have vanished. There'll be no visitors soon."

"I'm sure the royal family will think of another messy moneymaking venture to keep you on your toes." Evander slung an arm around my shoulders. "You'll always be wanted."

"Maybe it's good if I move on," I said. "Now we have three dragons to care for, things will only get busier. How are they?"

"They're doing well," Seraphina said. "Juniper is sick, but her presence is calming Stormwing."

"He's in love with her." Evander chuckled. "He hasn't said a single curse word since she arrived. And I haven't heard him break wind once."

Hodgepodge huffed out a breath. "It's a miracle."

Seraphina smiled. "Juniper is being a positive influence on him. But she's weak. And she keeps talking about her missing baby. It's the only thing she can focus on."

I looked at Finn. He nodded. Not so long ago, Finn had gotten himself into a serious situation involving a dragon egg that showed up at his animal sanctuary. It may be a coincidence, but it was rare for a dragon to misplace her egg. I had a feeling that Juniper was connected to the egg. If that was true, we knew exactly where her baby was and how she could get her back.

"Did I miss something?" Evander had noticed our silent exchange and looked at Finn with suspicion.

"It's a side project we need to deal with." I focused on Warwick. "Any news about the royal family?"

"Their unhappiness has never been so profound." Sharp joy traced his words. "They know the dragons are free, and they know sending a force of attack wraiths failed. They're working on another plan."

"Do you know what it is?"

"Not yet. The second I do, you'll all be informed."

"Be careful around them," I said. "They must know someone from their inner circle is feeding us information."

"I always am," Warwick said.

"We found an interesting puzzle when we went to collect what was left of Prince Godric," Astrid said.

"Don't tell me he'd reformed," I said.

She shook her head. "The pieces were gone."

"Did you look in the right place?"

"Of course!"

"He shattered. There were bits of stone everywhere. I'm sure I've still got some of him in my hair." I looked at Finn.

"He did. There'd be no way he'd come back from that." Finn pinched his chin between his thumb and finger, a pensive expression on his face.

"Did someone take the pieces?" I wasn't happy about that possibility. It meant we could have been seen with the dragons.

"What would anyone want with bits of a broken stone prince?" Evander lounged against the kitchen counter. "Your angel's magic must have turned him to dust, and he blew away on the breeze. Best place for him. He can't hurt anyone else while he's floating in the wind."

Astrid smirked. "Unless someone inhales a lung full of dusty prince and makes them cough."

Finn shrugged. "It's the first time I've used my magic like that, so anything's possible."

"Why didn't that happen to the other statues?" I asked.

"They were farther away and inside the castle? It's just a guess, but the impact of my magic wouldn't have been so strong from such a distance," Finn said.

"If he hadn't been such a twisted son of a gun, I'd almost feel sorry for Prince Godric," Griffin said. "Raised by an ice queen, belittled and overlooked because he was the younger son, and given a privileged life, he never had to deal with reality."

"Prince Godric deserves no forgiveness," Astrid said. "He wanted to turn us to stone and destroy us. He almost destroyed my baby Hodgepodge. And we can't have that." She scratched Hodgepodge's very much alive head.

Finn heaved himself out of the chair and stretched his wings.

"You stay back." Hodgepodge flared his neck ruff and hissed. "We've had enough of you."

"Finn is safe," I said.

"I'm no threat to anyone. I feel weary to my very marrow," Finn said. "It'll take me weeks to recover after Bell almost pounded me into oblivion. And did you have to throw me quite so hard into that tree, Hodgepodge?"

"You threatened Bell. It was no less than you deserved."

Finn nodded. "You did what you had to do, and I appreciate it. My demon had me around the throat, and he was choking the life out of me."

"I'll do it again if you overstep," Hodgepodge said.

"Heard and understood." Finn looked at me. "May I have a moment alone? Just the two of us?"

"Come here, Hodgie." Astrid scooped Hodgepodge off my shoulder. "You're overdue a belly rub. You deserve it for being so brave."

Hodgepodge didn't look happy about being left out as I led Finn out of the front door and gently eased it closed behind me. "What's on your mind?"

His affable smile and adorable dimples were back where they belonged. "I feel like I need to thank you a million times. I'd lost control. I wanted to destroy everything, you included."

"I knew the risks. And they were worth it. You freed Hodgepodge. We found out who killed Augustus. We finally destroyed Prince Godric and the stone heart amulet, and all the trapped people are free. Everyone got their lives back, and we've destroyed a dangerous person and a dangerous piece of magic."

"And your kiss brought me back," Finn said. "I always thought it was pain that gave me control, but..."

"I figured a kind surprise would work better."

Finn's eyebrows flashed up, and his smile faltered. "That was the only reason you kissed me?"

I repressed a grin. "You're thinking I was attracted to your demon side?"

Finn chuckled. "Some women like the bad boys."

"I don't. I like good people. Kind people. Those who help others. I kissed your demon because he needed a shock. I doubt anyone's ever shown him kindness."

"Yeah, most likely not." Finn's gaze caught mine, and we stared at each other for a few seconds. "That was some adventure."

"Yes, an unexpected one. I'm glad you were here to help." I dipped my gaze. "I suppose you'll be moving on now?"

Finn shook his head and took hold of my hand, drawing my gaze back to him. "If you'd like me to stick around, I'm happy to."

"What about looking for your mother?"

"I've been waiting to find her all my life. I can wait a little longer. And what's going on here is more urgent." He squeezed my hand. "Besides, I like spending time with you. And I want to find out what kissing you is like when I've not been taken over by a twisted demon who wants to destroy you, me, and the entire world."

I smiled, my cheeks hot as Finn slowly lowered his head.

The front door burst open, and Hodgepodge jumped between us, my lips meeting his side, as he kicked Finn back.

Astrid was right behind him, the rest of the gang looking at the scene and laughing.

"We'll continue this another time," Finn said.

"There's nothing to continue," Hodgepodge said. "You're leaving."

"No, Finn is staying," I said. "We need all the allies we can get, because this fight isn't over."

The laughter died, and expressions grew serious.

"What do we do next, Bell?" Griffin asked.

I looked at my battle-scarred friends as I lifted Hodgepodge and settled him on my shoulder. They were ready to continue the fight even though they knew the danger. My heart was so full of love that I couldn't speak.

"We eat cake," Hodgepodge declared. "We take a month off, sleep, eat, and ignore the troubles, just like we used to."

"I like some of that plan," I said, "but the dragons won't wait. Neither will the Ithric family."

"They'll be hunting their enemies," Warwick said. "We'll eventually make it onto that list."

"And we need to be ready when they find us," I said. "We get the dragons strong, make sure they can rule again, and we end the Ithric family's tyranny for good."

"Sounds like a plan," Evander said. "But I agree with Hodgepodge. First, we eat cake."

I returned to my lodgings with my exhausted, happy family. The fight wasn't over, but for now, it was time to eat cake and envelop all the laughter and love we could in readiness for the dark times to come.

Want to find out what's next for Bell and Hodgepodge?
Get Fireside and Shadow.
Read on to learn more.

Is this the end or the start of something magical?

Bell and Hodgepodge, find themselves thrust into the ultimate battle against the royal family's schemes. The dragons are awake, heralding danger and hope, while Bell grapples with her newfound abilities and the burden of an unforeseen destiny.

Entwined in a labyrinth of cunning spun by Lady Isolda, Bell navigates the twists and turns of a realm on the verge of upheaval. Unveiling the secrets within the castle's walls, she exposes the lengths to which Lady Isolda has gone to maintain her throne.

As Bell and Hodgepodge strive to protect loved ones and help the dragons, alliances are tested, and a battle for the soul of the realm unfurls. Will Bell master her magic in time to rescue her home, or will the lingering shadows of the past devour all she holds dear?

Find out in book 3 of the Fireside Mysteries – Fireside and Shadow.

About the Author

K.E. O'Connor (Karen) is the author of the whimsical
Fireside mysteries, the adorably fun Lorna Shadow
cozy ghost mystery series, the wickedly funny Crypt
Witch paranormal mystery series, the Magical Misfits
Mysteries featuring a sassy cat with a bundle of twisty
puzzles to solve, the slightly darker Witch Haven
paranormal mystery series featuring four troubled
witches and their wonderful furry (feathered and
web-slinging companions), and the delicious Holly
Holmes cozy baking mysteries.

Stay in touch with the fun mysteries:

Newsletter: www.subscribepage.com/cozymysteries
Website: www.keoconnor.com
Facebook: www.facebook.com/keoconnorauthor

Printed in Great Britain
by Amazon